Books by Tina Folsom

Out of Olympus

A Touch of Greek (#1)

A Scent of Greek (#2)

A Taste of Greek (#3)

A Hush of Greek (#4)

Werewolf Alliance

New Blood (#1)

Crimson Heart (#2)

Forbidden Mates (#3)

Scanguards Vampires

Samson's Lovely Mortal (#1)

Amaury's Hellion (#2)

Gabriel's Mate (#3)

Yvette's Haven (#4)

Zane's Redemption (#5)

Quinn's Undying Rose (#6)

Oliver's Hunger (#7)

Thomas's Choice (#8)

Silent Bite (#8 1/2)

Cain's Identity (#9)

Luther's Return (#10)

Mortal Wish (# 1/2)

Blake's Pursuit (#11)

Fateful Reunion (#11 1/2)

John's Yearning (#12)

Ryder's Storm (#13)

Damian's Conquest (#14)

Grayson's Challenge (#15)

Isabelle's Forbidden Love (#16)

Cooper's Passion (#17)

Vanessa's Bravery (#18)

Patrick's Seduction (#19)

Stealth Guardians

Lover Uncloaked (#1)

Master Unchained (#2)

Warrior Unraveled (#3)

Guardian Undone (#4)

Immortal Unveiled (#5)

Protector Unmatched (#6)

Demon Unleashed (#7)

Thriller: Eyewitness

Code Name Stargate

Ace on the Run (#1)

Fox in plain Sight (#2)

Yankee in the Wind (#3)

Tiger on the Prowl (#4)

Hawk on the Hunt (#5)

Venice Vampyr

Wicked Lover (#1)

Final Affair (#2)

Sinful Treasure (#3)

Sensual Danger (#4)

The Hamptons Bachelor Club

Accidental Escort (#1)

Accidental Truth (#2)

Accidental Scandal (#3)

Accidental Exposure (#4)

Accidental Imposter (#5)

Accidental Indiscretion (#6)

Time Quest

Reversal of Fate (#1)

Harbinger of Destiny (#2)

Harbinger of Destiny

Time Quest #2

Tina Folsom

1

No Woman, no Cry

Los Angeles, Friday, July 13, 2085

Joshua Fletcher cast a look at the full-length mirror of his closet door. He wanted to look good tonight. After all, he'd made an important decision, and now it was time to execute it. His entire family depended on him. He was the only male descendent of the Fletcher family, the only one capable of continuing the family's genes.

His female cousins, of which there were few to begin with, had all inherited the gene mutation that made them infertile. As a man, he wasn't affected by the gene, but it didn't make starting a family any easier. There were few women who could still bear children, even fewer who were even remotely in his age range. After all, as a twenty-two-year-old self-proclaimed stud, he didn't want to marry a woman ten years his senior.

Joshua smirked at his image in the mirror. Luckily, he'd met the right girl six months earlier. Not only was she two years younger than him, Kelly was also drop-dead gorgeous and one of the very few women who didn't carry the faulty gene and could therefore bear children.

His parents had been ecstatic when they'd met Kelly. They had encouraged him to take the next step quickly. After all, women like Kelly were a hot commodity, and despite his young age and the fact that he was still studying medicine, Joshua could offer her a good life. His parents were already eyeing a house to purchase for the young couple as a wedding present. And the subsidies a couple would receive when becoming parents would take care of the rest until Joshua was ready to enter the workforce as a medical doctor.

Kelly would never have to work a day in her life. Her purpose was to help repopulate the world. She was aware of her duty. Her parents had drilled it into her from the moment the gene test had determined that she was one of the lucky few. She was willing to fulfill her duty. Now all Joshua had to do was to make it official. Tonight, he would ask her to marry him.

It wasn't at all unusual for people as young as Joshua to get married. Ever since basic necessities such as healthcare, food, and—in some cases—shelter, had been guaranteed to every citizen in the world, young people everywhere, freed from student loans, got married and started a family much earlier than their parents and grandparents.

Joshua touched the mirror, deactivating it, and it turned back into the door to his closet. He left his room and walked downstairs. He liked the home he shared with his parents. Even though it was made from the same composite material all houses were made of in the 2080s, a mixture of stone and biodegradable waste, and 3D-printed by one of the many 3D construction companies, the style was uniquely early twentieth century: a Victorian home, yet with all the modern trappings of the 2080s.

While dating, his parents had toured the Museum of San Francisco, a one-square-mile open-air complex that housed original Victorian homes that had been restored after the great Tsunami had lain waste to a large part of the northern California city in

2037. They'd fallen in love with the architecture.

"Mom?" Joshua called out toward the kitchen when he stepped into the first-floor hallway.

"Hello, Joshua. Your mother is in the garden. Do you want me to ask her to come inside?" the house robot asked from one of the speakers in the house.

"No, thanks, Jeeves. I'll go outside myself."

"As you wish."

He rolled his eyes and walked into the kitchen. Sometimes Jeeves could be downright annoying, though the bodyless computer system that liked to be called by the name of a valet from the 1900s, did have its uses.

"Make yourself useful, and order me a car to pick up Kelly. I'll be leaving in five minutes."

"Yes, of course, Joshua."

The French doors to the deck and garden were open, and he saw his mother pruning her roses. He walked outside onto the deck.

"Is that what you're wearing for your date with Kelly?" The disapproval came from Jeeves.

"Zip it, Jeeves," he said and flipped him the bird.

By walking outside onto the deck, one of the outside cameras that acted as a security system had captured him. There were no cameras in the interior of the house. Just as well. Joshua liked his privacy. And there was nothing wrong with what he was wearing: a vintage pair of jeans he'd found in a costume store. Pants like that were hard to come by. And he rather liked the way he looked in them.

"Hey, Mom. I'm leaving."

His mother turned to him and smiled as she walked toward him. She was beautiful, her hair black as a raven's, her eyes a bright grey, her skin dark brown. His mother was the product of a mixed-race union, while Joshua's father was white. Marriages like his grandparents' and his parents' were very common. After the race riots in the early 2030s, wide-sweeping reforms had taken hold, and over the next two decades, racial equality was finally spreading to every corner of the world. In the world Joshua lived, race wasn't of consequence anymore, because once economic inequalities were removed, all that was left was one race: the human race. Everybody was pulling in the same direction to take mankind off the endangered species list. And Joshua would do what was within his power to save humankind from extinction. Luckily, this task involved his favorite pastime: having sex with Kelly.

"You remind me of when your dad and I were dating," his mother said, pointing at his pants. "You sure you want to wear that? I mean..." She hesitated and met his eyes. "This is an important night."

"I know what I'm doing." He chuckled. "Besides, Dad told me he was wearing jeans when he proposed to you. And it looks like that worked out fine."

His mother laughed softly. "Because we both love history and everything retro. But Kelly is different… uhm… more, I don't know… sophisticated?"

"It'll be fine, Mom, trust me." He leaned in and kissed his mother on the cheek. "Don't wait up for me. I'll stay over at Kelly's tonight." He winked at her. Celebrating their engagement in the only way he cared to: making love.

"Do you have the ring?" she asked.

"What ring?"

"The engagement ring, of course."

"You know as well as I do that you don't need a ring to propose marriage. It's expensive, and a total waste of resources. A wedding band will do just fine when the day comes."

"Yes, but…" She paused and motioned

him to follow her into the living room. "Kelly is a very beautiful young lady. It doesn't hurt to give her a little enticement." She opened the antique armoire and reached inside.

"Mom, that's really not—"

When she turned around, Joshua stopped himself. She was holding a tiny box in her hand. On its white velvet cushion sat a gold ring with a sparkling ruby as the center stone, surrounded by tiny diamonds.

"But that's from your grandmother," he said, shaking his head. "You can't... It's a family heirloom."

She smiled at him. "I don't see a better use for it than giving it to the woman who'll make sure our family continues."

Joshua wrapped his arms around his mother and hugged her tightly. "You're the best."

She sniffled and peeled herself out of his embrace. "Now, go, before I start crying." She pressed the box into his hand.

Joshua took it, closed it, and shoved it

into his jacket pocket. "I love you, Mom." Not wanting to get emotional in front of his mother, he pivoted and left the house.

The car he'd ordered was waiting at the curb. He let his gaze run over the vehicle. It wasn't the usual red or silver oval-shaped self-driving cab he normally got when he ordered transportation. It appeared that he'd been upgraded. While the shape was the same, it was white with silver accents, looking almost like a cloud. He'd have to have a serious word with his mother when he returned. She was trying to make him look like a knight in shining armor.

He doubted that Kelly would even understand this subtle nod to history. She wasn't interested in history. She was into fashion, music, and movies. She loved parties and vacations. She was enrolled in the local university, but Joshua wasn't even sure what major she'd chosen. Not that it mattered, because once they were starting a family, Kelly wouldn't have to get a job.

Joshua tapped his wrist to activate his holocom, and a hologram popped up and hovered over his left arm. He pointed it toward the car's lock, and the two devices communicated with one another.

"Welcome, Joshua," a female computer voice sounded from the car, and the door slid open.

Joshua entered and sat down in the comfortable seat. He tapped his holocom once more and the car door slid shut.

"Where to?"

"Kelly Shipley's house, please."

"Your estimated arrival time is 6:42 p.m.," the computer voice announced, and the car pulled into the street and merged with traffic.

"Would you like entertainment, Joshua?"

"Music from the 60s," he said and reclined his seat, closing his eyes to meditate to the music.

Techno-funk suddenly blasted from the

car's built-in speakers and made Joshua jerk up and almost hit the sunroof.

"Music from the *nineteen*-sixties," he demanded. The music stopped. Just to make sure the computer knew what he meant, he added, "Like the Mamas and the Papas."

"Calling your mama," the computer voice responded.

He already heard the dial tone. "No, don't call my mother." Sometimes, computers could be downright annoying. If he wanted something done right, it was best to do it himself.

"No music, no phone calls," he instructed the car's computer system.

Instead, he pulled up his holocom, tapped on his music library and synced it with the car's speakers. Moments later, the hippy sounds of a California band from the 1960s filled the car. The Beach Boys. He liked their vibe. He'd learned to appreciate their vintage sound from his father, and he understood why his father was such a fan, even though the band members themselves were long dead. The music always made him happy and carefree. And it was the perfect start for his life with Kelly.

Traffic was smooth. Through the tinted windows of the car, Joshua saw the landscape and other cars whizz past him, though he couldn't see who was inside the other vehicles. The windows had been designed to provide absolute privacy.

It didn't take long to reach Kelly's parents' house. In fact, he was almost twenty minutes early. But it didn't matter. He was eager to see Kelly and not afraid to show her his eagerness. Before he jumped out of the car, he told the car's computer to wait for him to return so the car could drive them to the small beachside restaurant where he would propose to her just as the sun set over the ocean.

The house that sat high on Mulholland Drive was modern, its 3D-printed materials forming a structure that looked like it was made of steel, glass, and concrete. From the driveway, the glass entrance door afforded a look into the enormous living room with a view over Los Angeles. He pressed the doorbell and waited. Moments later, Mrs. Shipley came into view. When she saw him, she froze for an instant, then marched to the door and opened it.

"Joshua?" she asked. "I wasn't expecting—"

"Hi, Mrs. Shipley, I know I'm early, but I can wait if Kelly isn't quite ready." He made a step toward her to enter, but she didn't move. In fact, she blocked him.

"Yeah, uh, about that..." She cast a nervous look down the hallway to where the kitchen and dining room were located.

"Is something wrong?" Joshua asked, a weird feeling spreading in his gut.

"Mom? Are you coming?" Kelly called out from the hallway. "We want to open the champagne." Kelly came into view. "We are

—" She abruptly stopped when her eyes fell on Joshua.

"Kelly..." he said, but his voice trailed off. She was dressed for their date, wearing a short azure-blue dress that accentuated her slim figure and her long blond hair that cascaded over her shoulders. The sight took his breath away.

"Joshua... uh..."

There was an undertone of something in her voice that he couldn't quite identify. It couldn't be a surprise. After all, she knew he was coming. Was it dread? Impossible. Still, her facial expression was one of discomfort. But why? She couldn't be sick. After all, she'd just mentioned opening a bottle of champagne. But why before the date? Had she guessed that he was planning to propose tonight?

All those questions raced through his mind in a millisecond.

Mrs. Shipley turned to Kelly. "I thought you sent him a message," she said low under her breath, though Joshua had no trouble hearing her.

"What message?" Joshua asked, his gaze ping-ponging from mother to daughter. Neither seemed to find the words to answer him.

Suddenly a man came from the hallway and appeared in the foyer. It wasn't Kelly's father, but rather a much younger man, perhaps ten years older than Joshua.

"Darling," he said and put his hand possessively on Kelly's lower back. "What's going on?"

That's when Joshua noticed it: the diamond ring on Kelly's finger. All air left his lungs. He stared at Kelly and the man whose arm was around her waist.

"Kelly?" But Joshua was unable to ask the question that lay on his tongue. Why ask it, when he already knew the answer?

"Corbin, why don't you and I join my husband on the terrace, and give Kelly a moment?" Mrs. Shipley said suddenly.

"Of course," the man said, and a moment later the two disappeared down the hallway.

"I'm sorry, Joshua," Kelly finally said. "You must have known that I... that you weren't the only one who..."

Frozen, Joshua clamped his jaw shut, fighting for self-control, fighting not to run after the bastard that had taken Kelly from him and beat him to a pulp. Instead, he glared at Kelly.

Kelly sighed. "I'm really sorry, Joshua... but—"

"But what?" he interrupted. "You played me. You used me to get a better offer. What was I to you? A prop?"

"It wasn't like that," she protested. "Corbin and I are just more compatible. Our families are in the same circles..."

That's when it clicked. He knew who Corbin was. Or rather, he knew about his family. Inside him, his heart was breaking.

"Save your breath! Why don't you just admit that he bought you! I'm not stupid.

The Carmichaels want their heir to have children, so they bought him a woman who can guarantee that their name lives on." He welcomed the anger fueling his words now. Better anger than showing her that she'd hurt him. "I hope you'll be happy with him."

He pivoted and left, not waiting for an answer.

2
Should I Stay
or Should I Go?

"Where to?" the car's driving system asked him.

For a moment, Joshua couldn't think. He didn't want to go home and have to admit to his parents that he'd failed and that Kelly had chosen somebody else over him. All these months, he'd simply been an accessory for her until she could attract a bigger fish. And one such fish had bitten and swallowed the bait hook, line, and sinker.

"Just drive around..." he said.

"Drive around? I can't find this destination. Please clarify."

"Just anywhere. I don't care, just not home," Joshua said impatiently.

"Did you mean a care home?"

"No! I don't fucking mean a care home. You're a moron, and I don't even know why I'm wasting my time talking to you. Your program sucks." Then he said, emphasizing every word as if talking to an idiot, "I want to travel to no particular place. And take your time. Get it?"

"Destination accepted. You will reach your destination in thirty-two minutes."

Finally, the car moved and merged into traffic. Joshua didn't bother looking at the display in front of him that indicated the destination. It didn't matter. All he wanted was to be alone for a while so he could think and wallow in his pain.

How could he have been so blind and not have seen that Kelly didn't love him? And she didn't even have the decency to tell him it was over. As if she'd completely forgotten that he existed. As if he didn't matter. Anger swapped places with his pain. How dare she treat him like that? He balled his hands into fists. He would make sure that this would never happen again. And the only way to guarantee it, was to never trust another woman when she told him that she loved him.

He tightened his jaw in determination. Nobody would ever play with his heart again, because he wouldn't allow anyone to get close to it. It was the only way to protect himself.

When the car suddenly slowed and pulled into a large parking lot, Joshua looked around.

"Where are we?"

"You've reached your destination."

"What destination?"

"The Institute for Time Travel as you requested," the car's computer announced.

"I didn't..." He stopped himself, recalling

what he'd said to the computer earlier. Had he inadvertently used words that the computer had misinterpreted? He shook his head. What did it matter?

He opened the door and stepped outside. He wasn't the only young man arriving in the parking lot and exiting a vehicle. Everybody was heading toward the main entrance where a long line had already formed.

A guy his own age walked past Joshua.

"Hey, buddy," he called out to the stranger.

The guy looked over his shoulder. "Yeah?"

"What's the line for?"

"Enrollment for the time-travel program. We'd better get in line fast, or we'll have to wait for another week."

The guy continued walking, and Joshua caught up with him and walked alongside him. "What's the program about?"

The young man cast him a quizzical look.

"Have you been living under a rock? They're recruiting young men to go back in time and bring back fertile women. I mean, that's why you're here, right?"

Not wanting to look like an idiot, Joshua said quickly, "Oh, sure, yeah, just wanted to make sure I'm at the right place. I didn't get a lot of information beforehand."

"Same. I'm Timothy, by the way."

"Joshua. So what else do you know about it?"

"Only that tonight's the sign-up, and then they'll give us a one-week orientation before they send us into the past."

Intrigued, Joshua asked, "Which year?"

"2025. Just before the virus."

Now it clicked. Joshua was aware that the virus that had eventually caused infertility in women had come from a pandemic in 2025. "Brilliant idea."

"Totally," Timothy said. "I've always wanted to know what life was like back then." He motioned to Joshua's pants. "Did your invitation say that you should come dressed for the period? Darn, I must have missed that. I'd better call my mother to see if she can rummage through the second-hand shops to find me a pair of jeans. Fuck, I hope they're not gonna reject me because I don't have the right outfit."

Timothy already pulled up his holocom, but before he could call his mother, Joshua nudged him. "I don't think you need to come dressed in jeans." They'd just reached the end of the line, and from what Joshua could see, nobody apart from himself was wearing a pair of jeans.

Everybody was wearing the loose-fitting and somewhat shapeless pants that were common in 2085.

As the line moved along rather swiftly, Joshua noticed the signs that were placed along the line. They contained a little bit more information about the time-travel program than Timothy had revealed.

"You will be sent back to March 2025

and be given six months to convince the woman assigned to you to travel back to 2085 with you," Joshua read. *"The one-week training will start on Monday and prepare you for your time in the past. Thank you for your service to humankind."*

"It's like a paid vacation, and I won't even have to take time off from my studies," Timothy said.

"What do you mean? You're gonna be gone for six months."

"Yeah, in the past. But when I come back, I'm coming back a day after I leave. Didn't you read that in the letter you got? It's basically just a one-week commitment. We travel to the past after the one-week orientation, and we'll come back here the day after, even though we'll have spent six months in the past."

"Now I get it," Joshua said. And maybe that was just what he needed: a six-month break from this world to get over Kelly. At the same time, he'd only be gone for a week, so his parents would barely have time to miss him. And he'd be serving humankind and do his part to repopulate the world. But...

"Do you think we'll have to marry the woman we bring back?" Joshua asked.

The guy in front of Joshua and Timothy turned around. "I heard that that's not a requirement. All we need to do, is to bring one back."

Joshua nodded. That suited him fine. "But we can fuck her, right?"

Timothy chuckled. "We'd better. I'm not going six months without sex."

Joshua nodded in agreement. "Yeah, me neither."

He thought about his current situation. He had nothing to lose. He had no girlfriend, and his parents would be disappointed that there would be no little Fletcher babies in the near future. His next semester didn't start for another two months, and the idea that he would nurse his broken heart for the next few months without anything to keep his mind off it, was unbearable. Why not get over Kelly while he was in the past, and then return as a new man, his feelings for Kelly eradicated? He needed a rebound relationship anyway, and could dump the woman once he was back. And since he wasn't expected to marry the girl he brought back, he didn't care who she was. Well, as long as she was fuckable enough.

By the time Joshua reached the front of the line, he'd made his decision.

"Name and Global ID Number?"

He recited both to the woman in the white lab coat who sat at a high table over which a hologram hovered.

"Ah, here you are," she said and tapped something on the virtual keyboard. "You didn't do your pre-registration."

"Uhm, yeah, I must have forgotten. It's not a problem, is it? I really want to be part of this."

She looked him up and down, when her

gaze caught on his pants. "Well, I guess at least you came prepared."

"Yes, ma'am."

He was ready for this adventure. An adventure in an era where everything seemed so much easier. He couldn't wait for this exciting journey into the past.

3
Only the Lonely

Santa Monica, Monday, March 24, 2025

Amy Brooks stuffed her books and papers into her backpack and slung it over her shoulder. Before she could head to the door, several of the other students at the Santa Monica Community College had already risen from their seats and were blocking the aisle.

"Excuse me," she said and tried to squeeze past them, but they didn't budge. "Can I please get through?"

Jennifer glanced over her shoulder.

"Can't you see that we're having a conversation?"

"I have to catch my bus."

But Jennifer clearly didn't care. Amy doubted that she'd ever been on a bus. After all, she had a car, something Amy could only dream of. But that's all it was, a dream.

She barely had enough money to pay for a tiny room in an apartment she shared with five others. She'd lived there for a year now, ever since she'd turned eighteen and had thus aged out of the foster care system. She was on her own. Her parents, two drug addicts who should have never had a child, deserted her when she was four, and ever since then she'd been passed from one foster family to the next.

At age ten, she'd given up any hope of ever being adopted. At age sixteen, she'd given up hope of ever being loved. But she wasn't ready yet to give up hope of making something out of herself. That's why she worked at an independent coffee shop, taking whatever shifts she could get, while attending classes at a community college to earn a degree so she could better herself.

But it was a daily struggle. She was still trying to navigate the complicated maze of student aid and student loans, and had to rely on her wages at the coffee shop to pay for her basic needs. When the tips were good, she managed to eat better food than just slices of pizza, but many days it was just that or whatever leftovers she could scrounge from the coffee shop. She wasn't too proud to squirrel away half-eaten muffins customers left on their plates. Pride didn't fill her belly. Pragmatism did.

Besides, nobody took any notice of her anyway. And when they did, it was only to recoil from her. She preferred it when they didn't even realize she was there, except for moments like this, when somebody blocked her way.

Amy couldn't wait any longer. With Jennifer and her friend still blocking the aisle, Amy stepped onto a chair, then from there onto the desk, then descended on the other side.

"Look at the monkey," somebody said, pointing at her, but she didn't look in the guy's direction.

She'd heard it all before. The words didn't hurt much anymore. They had at first, but she'd grown a stronger armor, and barely heard the insults or the mocking. She just ignored the people who were unkind to her and stepped into the aisle just past Jennifer, then hurried to the door.

"Freak," another guy called after her. Several others giggled, but Amy was already at the door and rushed outside.

She ran across the courtyard and toward the street. The bus stop was only a block farther. She ran, but the sidewalk was busy, and she had to dodge many people who were just meandering without a destination. When the traffic light turned red just before she reached the pedestrian crossing, she cursed. The blue bus was already at the bus stop and closing its doors. She wanted to cross the lanes of traffic, but couldn't. It would be suicide.

Frustrated, she looked at her watch. She knew the bus schedule by heart and knew that the next one wouldn't arrive for another twenty minutes. She couldn't wait that long, or she would be too late for her shift at the coffee shop. And there was one thing her employer was adamant about: punctuality.

He'd fired one of the other employees for tardiness only two weeks earlier. Amy knew that her fate would be the same if she was late. And she couldn't afford to lose her job. It meant losing her room too, because she had no money saved up to pay her rent. Whatever she made each month, she spent immediately. There was never anything left over. No chance to save a penny for a rainy day, because her life was one long, rainy day.

Knowing she'd land on the street if she

didn't make it to work on time, Amy took off running. With every block, her backpack felt heavier, and at every intersection she took more chances with her life. Maybe she had a guardian angel who was looking out for her, because despite the angry motorists honking at her, no car hit her. She took that as a good sign. Still, she couldn't allow herself to slow down. She was already sweat-bathed, despite the cool ocean breeze that started traveling into Santa Monica, providing cool evenings despite the southern California location.

By the time she finally reached the cute coffee shop, which was located only a few blocks from the main shopping area, Third Street Promenade, she was exhausted. She jerked the door open and entered. Her colleague Rosie stood at the counter, looking stressed. When Amy hurried toward her and tossed her backpack into the storage room behind her, Rosie said under her breath, "You're late!"

"I know, I'm sorry, but I missed the bus. Please don't tell Mr. Mercola. Is he here?"

Rosie sighed and untied her apron. "You're lucky. He called an hour ago to say that he won't be here to close up. You'll have to do that tonight." Rosie pressed a set of keys into her hand.

"But—"

"I can't stay, I'm sorry," Rosie said. "I have a dentist appointment." She looked at the clock on the wall. "And I'll be late if I don't hurry now. See you tomorrow." At the door, she cast a last look over her shoulder. "And don't worry, I won't tell Mercola that you were late. We've got to cover for each other, right?"

Amy nodded. "Right."

Rosie, who was one or two years older than Amy, had always been kind to her. Or perhaps Rosie pitied her. No matter. As long as she wasn't cruel, Amy considered it a win. The two other employees, Sandra and Gavin, were also comparatively young and could be obnoxious. Luckily, Amy rarely worked the same shifts as those two. She was fortunate that she was often paired up with Rosie. In a way, they'd even become friends in the last six months, even if they didn't hang out outside of work.

Mercola always employed young people without any experience so he could get away with paying only the bare minimum. No wonder there was a huge turnover of employees. Those who were able to find a better job left as soon as they could. Only Amy was a constant at the coffee shop. She had no other options. Most prospective employers took one look at her and rejected her application.

Amy tied the black apron around her waist and checked the display case of pastries and ready-made snacks. The glass-front refrigerator where the cold drinks were stored was almost empty. Rosie hadn't refilled it, even though it was part of her job. Amy sighed. Since Rosie wasn't lazy, it probably meant that her shift had been a busy one.

There were only a few customers at present, and they'd already been served and were nursing their coffees and pastries or whatever else they had ordered.

Amy restocked the fridge and display cases and tidied up behind the counter, before the early evening rush started. She preferred the café when it was busy. It meant that time passed quickly, and she didn't think too much about her lot in life. This day was no different. The café had its fair share of regulars but, because of its location close to Third Street Promenade, also a good amount of tourists. She preferred the regulars. They knew her, and by now didn't stare anymore. It was the tourists who stared, and kids that pointed at her, or worse, little kids that were scared at the sight of her and started crying. The embarrassment of the parents was often followed by a hasty retreat.

Amy tried everything to make her appearance less conspicuous. She'd stopped wearing her hair in a ponytail though it would be more sanitary in the coffee shop. Instead, she'd learned to tilt her head to one side so her long hair fell into her face, covering what she herself had stopped looking at in the mirror.

When it got quieter, and the few customers left in the shop were sitting at the few small tables, Amy pulled out her sketchpad and started drawing. She'd always loved drawing, even as a child, but in the last three years, drawing had become an escape for her. Her sketchpad was filled with pencil drawings depicting other worlds. When she drew the pictures that she saw before her mental eye, she imagined living in another place, another world, where life was easier, where someone loved her, where she could be happy. And for a while she was transported away to her fantasy world.

One day, she would take the pictures in

her sketchpad and spin a story around them, perhaps make a graphic novel out of it. And perhaps the graphic novel would help others in the same situation as hers gain hope that one day things would turn out all right. She'd never shown the drawings to anyone. This was her world, her secret, the one thing nobody could take away from her. Nobody could criticize it or destroy it. This was what got her through her lonely days and nights.

At nine o'clock, closing time, the last customer finally left, and Amy locked the door behind him, then cleared the tables and cleaned up. During her shift, she'd put leftovers that looked almost untouched into a container. There was one half of a tuna sandwich, a muffin that the customer had only taken one bite of, and a cup of fruit. This would be her lunch the next day. She'd rarely ever taken any of the food from the display cases or the refrigerator, other than a slice of bread or cheese. One of the previous employees had warned her that

Mercola kept a close eye on all supplies. Pilfering them would get her fired.

Once she'd cleaned up, she went back to the counter and emptied the tip jar. She counted the money, and then exchanged the coins for banknotes. It wasn't much. The tourists hadn't been very generous, knowing they'd never come back. The regulars tipped better, but Monday was always a slow afternoon and evening. It would have to do. At least she didn't have to buy any food today or tomorrow. She still had some leftover pizza in the fridge at home, which she'd eat tonight. And the doggie bag she'd made for herself would be her lunch tomorrow.

It was a little past nine o'clock when she turned off the lights and locked the door behind her. Tired, she walked toward the bus stop. Before she reached it, she noticed a man sitting on the ground, leaning against the door to a small boutique. She'd seen him many times before. He was homeless.

"Evening, young lady," he greeted her like always.

She smiled at him. "Evening." She caught his gaze zero in on the food container in her hand.

"Can you spare some food? Just a little?" he asked, his voice almost timid.

She sensed that he hated begging, and he rarely asked her, even though he often saw her walk by with food in her hand. Their eyes met, and in that moment, she knew he needed the food more than she did.

Amy approached him and bent down, placing the container in his lap. "Here, it's not much, but it's good. I had some earlier," she lied, while her stomach growled in protest.

"Thank you," he said with a smile. "God bless."

"Have a good night," she said and turned around to see her bus approach. She got on it and closed her eyes until she reached her destination. The apartment she shared with five other girls was in a large apartment building in Westwood, close to UCLA's campus. She would have loved to attend the university, but her meager funds only allowed her to attend a community college.

Don't reach for the stars, Amy, she warned herself, *or you might get burned.*

Arriving at the apartment, she went straight to the kitchen to heat up the pizza slices she kept there. She opened the fridge, but the box was gone. She turned around, looked at all surfaces, but it was nowhere to be found. With dread she opened the trash, and there, torn up, lay the cardboard box, empty.

She heard a sound from the door and looked up. Paula, one of her roommates stood there. "What happened to my pizza?"

"I'm a vegetarian, I didn't eat it." The girl shrugged. "Tracy's boyfriend was here earlier. He might have eaten it."

Amy's jaw tightened.

"What's the big deal anyway? That pizza

was already two days old." Then Paula just turned around and left the kitchen.

Amy just stood there, forcing down the tears that welled up. Frustration, helplessness, and hunger collided inside her. Today, she didn't have the strength left to fight her emotions, to fight the anger and the injustice. She made it to her room and locked the door, before tears ran down her cheeks like a flash flood. She didn't fight them any longer. She was too tired to fight. Tomorrow, she would start again, but tonight, she allowed herself to be weak and wallow in her pain.

4
Enter the Time Traveler

Santa Monica, Wednesday, April 2, 2025

Joshua Fletcher had arrived in Los Angeles a week earlier. He was in no rush to make contact with the woman assigned to him. She wasn't going anywhere. Instead, he used the time to get himself set up. He used his charm and the corporate payment apps he'd been issued to secure a cool studio apartment with a partial ocean view just off San Vicente Boulevard, where boutiques and restaurants lined the broad street.

From the apartment, he could walk to all

amenities, which was important, because he'd never learned to drive a car. The one-week training on life in 2025 hadn't included driving lessons. Very few people still knew how to drive a car. Since cars were self-driving in 2085, there was no need for it. It was a shame though, because when he looked at the different cars driving down the streets of Santa Monica, particularly those that had no roof—which were apparently called convertibles—he would have liked to experience what it was like to feel the wind in his hair while driving around without a destination.

Cruising, he'd overheard a group of young guys his own age call it. Or rather, *cruising for chicks*. Apparently, cars in 2025 were chick magnets. Maybe he should get one. It couldn't be all that hard to drive. Besides, he had a California driver's license. A fake one, but it would pass muster. The more Joshua thought about it, the better the idea sounded.

Why the instructors at the Institute for Time Travel hadn't thought of this was beyond him. After all, his mission was to seduce a young woman so she would travel to the future with him. This meant that he had to be more desirable than his competition, and from what he'd observed so far, every eighteen-year-old guy in Los Angeles had a car. It wouldn't exactly be sexy if Joshua went on a date with the woman assigned to him using a bus. What was her name again?

In the privacy of his apartment, Joshua tapped on his wrist and opened up his holocom, the communication device every person over the age of five wore. A hologram popped up and hovered over his arm. There she was: Amy Brooks. She was pretty in a girl-next-door kind of way. The few pictures he'd been able to download to his holocom before his departure were taken when she was fifteen or sixteen years old. Dr. Mandell, the instructor who'd gone over the details of his mission, had told him that no other photographs of the girl were available. Apparently, she wasn't active on social media, and didn't have a driver's license or passport.

However, the picture Joshua now looked at showed promise. By now, at age nineteen, Amy should have bloomed into a pretty woman, not stunningly beautiful, not like Kelly, but maybe that was better. Stunningly beautiful women could turn into cold-hearted ice princesses. Joshua had no intention of dealing with somebody like that ever again. This time he would be the one to terminate the relationship, not the woman.

But first things first.

It wasn't hard to find a car dealership. There were plenty along Wiltshire Boulevard in Santa Monica. However, he realized very quickly that purchasing a brand-new car was out of the question. The prices were beyond the limit allowed on his payment apps, a limit the technical staff at the Institute for

Time Travel had set. It was meant to protect the time travelers from being exposed.

The payment apps were linked to large corporate accounts in existence in 2025. They had been chosen from an array of companies whose accounting methods were less than stellar and where charges would remain undetected for months, before getting flagged for fraud. Because fraud it was. However, there was no other way for the time travelers to finance their stay, since very little paper money printed before 2025 was still available in 2085.

With a new car out of his price range, Joshua went to the first used-car dealership he found. *Rick's Rides* the sign said. Joshua walked into the lot with several rows of various cars parked close together. Big signs with prices in the windshield of each car made it easy to narrow down his choices.

"You look like a man on a mission."

At hearing the male voice, Joshua whirled around. A balding man in blue pants and a checkered jacket approached, his hand stretched out in greeting. Joshua hesitated. In the future, people didn't shake hands anymore. It curbed spreading diseases. But humankind in 2025 hadn't learned that lesson yet.

The man didn't seem to mind that Joshua didn't shake his hand and smiled instead. "I'm Rick. What can I help you with?"

"I'm looking for something... you know... for cruising."

"Ah, of course, I think I have the right thing for you. A total bargain. And in such good shape." Rick waved at Joshua to follow him to the far corner of the lot. "There it is. I haven't sold it yet, because I'm waiting for the right person. Somebody who'll appreciate the beauty of this car. A young man like you."

Joshua looked at the vehicle. It was red with a black roof made of a thick cloth-like material.

"Ah, I can see how you're looking at it. Love at first sight, right?" Rick chuckled. "Let me show you how it looks with the roof down." Moments later, the car salesman sat in the car, switched on the engine, and then made the roof lift up and slide into a compartment in the trunk.

"Wow," Joshua said. This was exactly what he was looking for.

"Nice, right? Wanna sit in it?"

Joshua nodded and changed places with the salesman. The seat was low for his tall frame, but he liked the feel of the leather cradling his back. He put his hands on the steering wheel and looked out through the windshield, where the price was written.

Rick removed the cardboard with the price. "It's a steal."

Joshua stared at the price. It was still too high. He motioned to it. "I'm afraid I don't have that much."

"You seem like a really nice young man.

Why don't I make you a deal? How about I knock off a thousand?"

Stunned, Joshua stared at Rick. "Are you sure? I mean..."

Nobody in 2085 would simply give somebody a discount. A price was a price. There was no haggling, no back-and-forth. Prices were set to the fair value of goods, no matter in which country or city they were offered. Price gouging was unheard of, though there was one area where prices could go sky-high and were subject to negotiation: adoptions.

Whenever a young woman found herself pregnant and didn't want to keep the child— or couldn't—, instead of getting an abortion, an adoption agency would step in to find the right parents for the child. The pregnant woman would be richly compensated and cared for in every way. It was a win-win for all parties involved.

Rick patted him on the shoulder. "What do you say? Do we have a deal?"

Before the salesman could withdraw his offer, Joshua gripped his hand and shook it. "I'll take it."

A half hour later, Joshua was the proud owner of a red Mini Cooper convertible. He jumped into the car and inserted the key into the ignition. When he turned the key, the engine came to life. He pressed the gas pedal down, the engine revved, but the car didn't move.

"You're in park," Rick, who stood next to the car, said.

Not wanting to look stupid, Joshua nodded. "Yeah, I know." Of course, he was parked. What the hell was the guy talking about? "Drive." But the verbal command didn't produce any movement either.

Joshua felt the salesman's gaze on him, which made him even more nervous. He felt heat rise up his torso into his head. Fuck, why didn't this car move?

"The gear shift," Rick said, pointing to

the black stick between the two front seats that looked similar to a dildo.

Joshua looked closer and noticed the letters that were etched on the metal base around the gear shift. P, R, D, N they said.

"You've gotta put it in drive," Rick now added, his voice carrying a good deal of doubt.

Figuring that D stood for drive, Joshua followed the instruction. Still, the car didn't move.

"And take the foot off the brake and put it on the gas pedal..."

The moment Joshua took his foot off the brake pedal and pressed down on the gas pedal instead, the car shot forward. He slammed on the brakes again, preventing the car from hitting another one by a hair's breadth.

"Shit!" Rick cursed. "Are you drunk?"

"No! Of course not!"

"Then what the fuck is wrong with you?"

Joshua glared at the salesman. "I'm not

used to driving a manual car." There! He'd admitted it.

"It's an automatic!" Rick said in a raised voice.

The guy was clearly lying. "What's automatic about having to operate it yourself?"

Rick shook his head. "I think you'd better get outta here before you damage any of my cars. And I'd advise you to take driving lessons."

Feeling humiliated, Joshua scrambled to make a turn to drive out of the dealership's lot. Apparently, driving a car wasn't quite as easy as he'd expected it to be.

It took him the rest of the day to feel comfortable driving his new acquisition. By the time the sun set, he parked the car outside his apartment building. He went upstairs and took a shower, then headed out again, this time on foot. He'd had enough of driving for one day. It was time to seek out Amy.

5

The Ugly Duckling

The Happy Grind coffee shop where, according to the historical records, Amy worked part-time was located a fifteen-minute walk away from Joshua's studio. He didn't know which shifts Amy worked, but he needed to check out the place anyway to get a feel for his surroundings so he could decide how to approach her.

The coffee shop was different from the others Joshua had frequented during his first week in 2025. Furnished with a mishmash of wooden chairs and tables, all of them rather antique looking, it exuded an air of an era long gone. On the walls hung old black-and-white photos of women and men, many of them autographed. Behind a counter, two employees were working. The man was restocking a refrigerator with bottled drinks, while the woman had her back turned and was busy cleaning out a coffee machine.

There were a few customers. A sign on the counter said *Please order here*. Joshua walked up to it, and the man approached from the other side.

"Evening, what can I get you?"

Joshua hadn't even thought about what to order. His eyes fell on the large blackboard on the wall behind the counter, where a menu had been written in colored chalk.

"Uh, I'll have an orange juice and..." He looked at the display of pastries. "...a blueberry muffin."

"Right away." The man turned to snatch a

small bottle of juice from the fridge, then put a muffin on a plate, when his cell phone chimed. He glanced at it. "Excuse me for a moment." He turned away, then addressed the woman cleaning the coffee machine. "Amy, please ring up this customer." He pointed to his phone. "I've gotta take this call."

"Sure, Mr. Mercola." She wiped her hands on a towel, while the man left through a door marked *Employees Only*.

Joshua's heart beat into his throat. This was Amy Brooks. He hadn't expected to see her on his first visit to the coffee shop. He wasn't prepared. Shit, had he even looked in the mirror before leaving his studio to see whether his hair wasn't standing in all directions? Were his clothes clean?

Fuck, he hadn't thought this through. The first impression was always the most important, and he hadn't even given it a thought. But it was too late to fix it now. He had to make the best of it.

Joshua planted a big smile on his face, ready to meet Amy and charm her from the moment she laid eyes on him.

She turned and glanced up at him for a brief second, before starting to type something on the tablet that acted as the register.

Joshua's smile froze on his lips. Shock coursed through him, paralyzing his body, while his heart raced uncontrollably. What the fuck? This couldn't be Amy Brooks. Somebody had made a mistake. Maybe he'd heard wrong when the man had asked Amy to ring up his purchase. It had to be. He frantically searched for names that rhymed with Amy, but his mind was blank. Then his gaze fell on the nametag the young woman wore on her shirt. *Amy B* it said. What were the odds of two Amys working in the same small coffee shop and both their last names starting with a B? Only a fool would bet on those odds. And he was no fool.

"That'll be $8.56." She turned the tablet toward him and looked up.

He saw it more clearly then. And he saw the resemblance to the photos he'd seen of her when she was younger. This was Amy Brooks, no doubt. Her eyes were of an unusual green, something akin to a cat's eyes, beautiful and mesmerizing. Her hair was dark, almost black, and looked like the most luxurious silk.

Joshua swallowed hard, unable to say or do anything. Anger churned up in him, and he recalled a moment during his one-week training at the Institute for Time Travel, where he'd been embarrassed in front of the entire group of time travelers.

Los Angeles, Friday, July 20, 2085

"We need you to travel back to before the outbreak of the virus," Professor Henley said, "to find those women of childbearing age who according to the historical records, died from the disease. We need you to find them, befriend them, romance them—hence Romeos—and bring them to our time, to 2085, before they can get infected and become worthless to us. Questions before I go on?"

Many hands went up, including Joshua's.

Professor Henley pointed to him. "You." He glanced at the nametag. "Joshua Fletcher."

"Why can we only bring back women who died during that pandemic? Wouldn't we have a better choice if we widened our criteria? I mean, what if they're all ugly?"

There was laughter behind him.

Professor Henley narrowed his eyes. "Because you want to return to the world you left, don't you? You want to come back to this version of 2085, not another."

The professor looked into the crowd, then sighed. "If you had listened to Mrs. Dorchester who explained quantum physics and the space time continuum to you, you wouldn't be staring back at me like clueless fish."

He paused for effect. "Well then. A refresher. If you were to pluck one random woman out from 2025 and transplant her to 2085, you will have changed the course of history. Imagine this woman was going to have a child, who then went on to make an important discovery in medicine, physics, chemistry, city planning, or even art. The absence of that person, that child and its descendants, would mean that our future, the world we live in right now, would become different. You will have created a new timeline, one in which your loved ones might not exist."

"You mean like if Albert Einstein's mother were to come back with one of us before she gave birth to him?" one recruit called out.

"Exactly. We've carefully selected from the pool of women who died during the

2025 pandemic, so we won't have to worry about a disruption in the space-time continuum. Only the women destined to die may be brought back to our time. It is the only rule you may never break, no matter the circumstances."

Then he looked at Joshua. "No matter how ugly the woman assigned to you is."

Joshua felt heat suffuse his neck and head. Shit! He'd never felt so embarrassed in his entire life. He could hear the snickering behind him, but there was no escape. His only consolation was that he would soon be traveling to another time where nobody knew him.

Santa Monica, Wednesday, April 2, 2025

The reason why Dr. Mandell hadn't provided him with newer photos of Amy became clearer with every second. Dr. Mandell and Professor Henley had decided to teach him a lesson, to punish him for his —admittedly insensitive—question.

They had paired him with a woman who could never be considered beautiful, not even pretty. No, they'd assigned him a woman whose left side of her face was marred by ugly scars that looked like burn marks—whether caused by fire or acid, he didn't know. It didn't matter. All that mattered was the result.

The pretty fifteen- or sixteen-year-old girl who'd once shown such promise of blooming into a beautiful young woman, looked grotesque. Whatever accident she'd had, had destroyed her good looks.

"How would you like to pay?" Amy asked, her voice a little sharper now, her gaze connecting with his.

He realized that he'd been staring at her for more than just a second. But she didn't look away. She tilted up her chin as if in defiance, as if daring him to look closer. He felt like a jerk.

"Apologies, my mind was somewhere else," he lied and reached for his wallet. For today he'd already taken out the maximum allowed from his digital payment source, so he pulled out a twenty-dollar-bill and handed it to her.

Amy opened a drawer underneath the counter and counted out his change. When she handed it to him, and he reached for it at the same time, their hands touched for a second. Instantly, Joshua pulled back. At the same time, he met her eyes. He knew immediately how she'd interpreted his action: as if he was disgusted by her, as if her touch was poisonous.

"I'm sorry," he said, quickly averting his eyes, unable to bear her hurt look any longer. Fuck! This wasn't a good start. Things couldn't get any worse.

Amy pushed the plate with the muffin and the bottle of orange juice toward him.

"Thank you," he said, then saw a plastic tip jar with coins and banknotes in them. He dropped the change she'd given him into it, not caring that his tip was larger than his bill.

Quickly, he grabbed his food and drink and retreated to a table in the far corner of the coffee shop. He took one bite from the muffin, but had lost his appetite.

6
I Will Survive

The young man who couldn't be older than twenty-one or -two stared at her with disgust in his eyes. Amy knew that look all too well. For three years she'd had to endure it from any number of people she encountered. Nobody had ever been able to look past the disfiguring scars to see the girl beneath the ugliness. She'd been popular in junior high, had made friends easily despite coming from a broken home and moving from one foster family to another. But ever since the event that had left her with scars so ugly that she rarely looked in the mirror anymore, everybody avoided her. As if she didn't deserve friendship or a kind word.

Or love...

She'd never before seen the young man who'd ordered a muffin and orange juice and was now digging into his pocket to pull out his wallet. It gave her time to study him. And why shouldn't she? He'd overtly scrutinized her as if she were a freak in the circus, or an exhibit in a museum.

He was tall, dark, and so very different from her. Too good looking. Too perfect. Too unattainable. But that didn't stop her from letting her eyes and her mind wander. His shirt clung to him, indicating the muscular physique beneath. His arms looked strong and could cradle a woman in need of protection. His eyes were dark brown, his nose straight, his dark hair short, his skin flawless. Yes, he was the kind of guy haunting any lonely girl's dreams. And that's all he would do, because a guy like this would never touch a girl like her.

The only time she ever felt a man's arms around her, his lips on her, his cock inside her, was when she went to a dark bar or nightclub—if there was no bouncer to get past—and picked up a guy who was too drunk to care or notice that she was ugly. Her favorite holiday was Halloween, because it was the only night where she could wear a mask that disguised her face, giving her an opportunity to meet others without them recoiling from her.

Amy accepted the twenty-dollar-bill the stranger handed her and counted out the change. She thrust the money toward him, and their hands touched. A jolt akin to an electrical charge went through her, making her keenly aware how much she missed being touched by a man, how much she craved affection and physical closeness. And that the man whose hand she'd touched flinched.

"I'm sorry," he mumbled.

Amy didn't acknowledge his words, didn't react, just pushed the plate with the muffin and the bottle of juice closer to him so he would withdraw and leave her alone with the longing that was spreading inside her now.

"Thank you," he said, then suddenly dropped the change she'd given him—all eleven dollars and forty-four cents—into the tip jar.

He turned quickly and walked to a table in the corner. She followed him with her eyes, allowing herself another second or two to daydream, before she turned back to cleaning the coffee machine.

Minutes later, Mr. Mercola was back. He shoved his cell phone into his pocket and looked at her.

"That was Donna. I need to leave. Can you close up tonight?"

She knew it wasn't a question, it was an order. She nodded, even though she didn't like the responsibility nor the fact that having to lock up meant she'd get home even later. "No problem, Mr. Mercola."

"Thanks, Amy."

He took off his apron and hung it on a hook in the employee closet. Amy turned back to cleaning the machine. She heard the sound of coins clinking and looked over her shoulder. Mercola fished a ten-dollar bill from the tip jar. When their eyes met, he said, "I need some change. I'll put it back tomorrow."

He headed out the door. Tears rose to her eyes, but she pushed them back. This wasn't the first time that he'd taken money from her tip jar, claiming he needed change and promising her he'd put it back the next day. He had yet to keep that promise. He'd never replaced the money he'd taken. Maybe he believed that as the owner he deserved the tips more than his employees. And what was she to do? Remind him that he hadn't put the tips back? If she did, he'd fire her, she was sure.

The coffee shop emptied out over the next hour, while Amy tidied up and cleaned what needed to be cleaned so she wouldn't have to stay too long after locking the door. The last person to leave was the handsome young man. When he walked to the door and opened it, he seemed to hesitate for a moment. He turned halfway, but then seemed to think better of it, and left.

Amy walked to the door, flipped the dead bolt and turned the sign from open to closed. Then she walked to the table the handsome stranger had occupied. The juice bottle was empty, but he'd taken only one bite from the blueberry muffin.

She pulled a small plastic bag from her apron's pocket and put the muffin into it. It would be her breakfast tomorrow. She took the empty bottle and straightened, while she looked out at the sidewalk. She froze. The young man who'd barely touched his muffin stood there, looking at her. He'd seen that she'd taken the leftover food, and while there was nothing wrong or illegal about taking food that somebody else had discarded, she felt embarrassment flood her. In the past three years she'd never cared what others thought of her, so why did it bother her now that this guy had witnessed her scrounge for food? Was it because it emphasized the chasm between him, a guy who seemed to have everything, and her, a girl who had nothing?

And soon, Amy would have less than nothing. Her rent was due in three days, and if she didn't tighten her belt even more, and if Mercola pilfered her tips again over the next few days, she wouldn't have enough to make the rent. She would be out on the street. And that prospect scared her.

She cast a defiant look at the man outside. She couldn't allow herself to feel embarrassed for being poor. She had to survive.

7
Do the Right Thing

Saturday, April 5, 2025

Amy snuck out of the apartment before any of her roommates had gotten up. She didn't need another confrontation with them. She hadn't been able to scrape enough money together to make the rent on the first of the month. Her roommates had grudgingly granted her a five-day extension, covering the rent for her until tonight. But then she would have to pay, or they would lock her out and have somebody else move in. It wasn't that they were trying to be mean to her, but since they too were on limited budgets, it wasn't easy for them to pay the full rent to the landlord when one roommate couldn't pay.

She had called her colleague Rosie and begged her to take on one of her weekend shifts at the coffee shop, and Rosie had done her the favor. It meant Amy would have two shifts today. On the weekend, the tips were generally better, and she was confident that she would be collecting sufficient tips to scrape together the rest of the rent money.

As predicted, most of the day it was busy in the coffee shop, and Amy had little time to take a breather. When it got quieter toward the early evening, the handsome stranger was back. He'd been back every day this week. She'd found out his name, Joshua, because on two occasions he'd paid with the app on his cell phone. And every time he'd left a large tip in cash.

Every time she served him, he addressed

her by her name and thanked her with a smile, just like he did now.

"Thanks, Amy."

Joshua flashed her a bright smile, and for a moment, she forgot about her scars and allowed herself to think that he was flirting with her. Of course, he wasn't, but it felt good to pretend that she was just like any other pretty nineteen-year-old single girl. To pretend that somebody was attracted to her.

His usual table in the corner was occupied by a young tourist couple, so he took a seat at a table near the door and set down his drink and pastry. As always, Joshua was alone. She'd never seen him with anybody or even talk on the phone to anyone. It surprised her. A guy with his looks and obvious charm had to be popular. And for sure somebody like Joshua had a girlfriend. And even if he didn't, Amy knew not to reach for the stars.

When the next customer paid with a

large bill and change was running low in the till, Amy exchanged the coins and smaller bills in the tip jar with larger banknotes and closed the till again. When she looked up, two new customers stood in front of her, ready to order.

"What can I get you?" she asked the two guys who seemed to be in their mid-twenties.

"I'll have a large latte, a grilled cheese panini, and a banana," the taller of the two said.

"I'll have the same," the second one added, "but I'd like my latte with non-fat milk."

Knowing that the sandwich took a few minutes on the panini grill, she said, "Let me get the sandwiches started for you right away. And then I'll ring you up."

Amy turned around and bent down to the refrigerator that held the sandwiches ready to be grilled and placed two of them on a plate using tongs. Then she rose and took a step toward the grill, when she heard a scraping sound coming from the counter. She glanced over her shoulder.

To her shock, she saw the shorter of the two guys snatching all the bills from the tip jar and stuffing them into his pocket, while the taller one blocked the other customers' view.

"Thief!" she yelled and charged toward them, while the plate with the sandwiches slipped out of her hand and dropped to the floor, shattering.

The two guys spun around and sprinted toward the door. Still behind the counter, Amy lost valuable seconds to run around it, when the shorter guy suddenly tripped and fell face forward. The other guy stumbled, but didn't fall.

"Fuck!" the one on the ground cursed, while the other one tried to get past him to escape.

But a fist struck him in the face and made him jerk sideways. When Amy had rounded the counter, she saw who'd struck the thief: Joshua. She realized immediately that the shorter guy hadn't tripped on his own. Joshua had tripped him.

Joshua now kicked the guy on the ground. "Give the money back!" he growled, while blocking the door so neither of the two thieves could escape.

Meanwhile, the few remaining customers stared at the melee. When the taller thief who was still standing tried to strike Joshua, Joshua pounded his fist into the guy's face and made him sway.

"I said give the fucking money back!"

Speechless, Amy watched as the guy on the floor reached into his pocket and pulled out the banknotes he'd stolen. Joshua snatched the money.

"If I ever see you guys again, you're dead!" Joshua warned, while the taller one helped his friend up.

"You should call the police," a customer

barked, while the two thieves scrambled to get out the door.

"It's handled," Joshua replied calmly and nodded to the customer who'd spoken up.

Then he bent down and picked up one of the banknotes that had fallen out of the thief's pocket in his haste to escape Joshua's wrath. He made two steps toward Amy, holding the money in his hand.

"Are you all right?" he asked.

"I should ask you that," she said. "You helped me."

The magnitude of his actions made her heart beat faster. If Joshua hadn't gotten the tip money back, she wouldn't have enough money to pay her rent and would be out on the street by tomorrow. Tears suddenly welled up in her eyes.

"It's all good now," he said.

"I don't know how to thank you. If you hadn't stopped them..."

He smiled and stretched out his hand. "Here, you'd better put that in your pocket."

Grateful, Amy took the money and shoved it into her apron's pocket. "You have no idea what this means to me."

"I'm glad I could help."

He reached for her arm and squeezed it briefly. The physical contact broke the last dam that was holding back her tears. She spun around, not wanting anybody to see her cry, particularly not Joshua. She didn't want to appear hysterical in front of him. And she realized why: she cared about what he thought of her.

8
A Hard Day's Night

Joshua watched Amy's shoulders quiver as she sobbed quietly. He'd spent the last week reading every little thing about her that he could find in the records he'd downloaded before his time jump. He understood her financial struggles, and if he needed any confirmation as to how bad her situation was, he only had to remind himself of what he'd witnessed: Amy had taken his half-eaten discarded muffin to eat.

The excitement he'd felt about traveling to the *good old times* was gone. These weren't the good old times. These were barbaric times. No human should have to scrounge for food. He'd seen plenty of homeless, mostly men, but also women, sleep on the sidewalks of Santa Monica, and was appalled by the callousness of the people of this era as they stepped around them rather than help them. But Joshua hadn't been sent to this time to help the homeless. He'd come to offer Amy a way out of her situation. He doubted that she would refuse if only he could bring himself to befriend her.

But it was easier said than done. Every time he looked at her, the scarred side of her face seemed more prominent than anything else about her. What would it be like to kiss her? He couldn't imagine it. He'd only ever been with beautiful girls, had never given a second thought to those not considered pretty. He knew he would at some point have to force himself to get close to her. And now was as good a time as any.

"Why don't I help you clean up the mess?" he asked. "I think those sandwiches need to be tossed." Joshua glanced behind the counter where the sandwiches had landed in a puddle of coffee that had spilled from a tray with dirty dishes.

"Oh my God, the sandwiches. My boss will find out that they weren't paid for. And I can't sell them now."

The tone in her voice told him that she feared reprisals from her employer.

"Why don't you charge them to me?"

She turned around and wiped her tears away. Her eyes red and puffy, she shook her head. "No, I can't let you do that. You've already helped me more than anybody."

"I insist."

"I can't accept that."

He couldn't help but smile. "Are you always this stubborn?"

"I'm not stubborn." She braced her hands on her hips and tipped up her chin.

Defiance. He liked that. She was no pushover. It shouldn't surprise him. She had to rely only on herself. Hardship had made her strong... and turned her into the polar opposite of Kelly.

"I guess then I'll just have to leave you a bigger tip than usual."

Her chin dropped. "You're already tipping more than any other customer."

He shrugged. "I like the service here."

For the first time, Amy smiled at him. "Your standards can't be very high."

Joshua winked at her. "Do you always insult your best customers?"

Amy blushed, and all of a sudden, she looked different. He couldn't put his finger on it, but her eyes seemed to beam, and the corners of her mouth curved up. She looked... happy.

Did it really take so little to make Amy happy, a few kind words, a smile, and some friendly banter? But would it be enough? Would it be sufficient to become her friend to convince her to come to the future with him? Or did he have to become her lover? It was a prospect that he didn't exactly relish. How could he become her lover when looking at her didn't arouse him?

It was best not to think that far. After all, he had nearly six months to decide how to approach the subject of time travel.

"I should get back to work," Amy suddenly said into the silence that stretched between them.

"You're not gonna let me help you, are you?"

She shook her head. "You already helped me. I can't ask you for anything else."

"You're not asking. I'm offering."

She gave him a long look. "I'm not used to relying on others."

Joshua had figured as much. He motioned to his table. "If you change your mind, I'll be right there."

She nodded and went back behind the counter, where she picked up the broken plate and the spoiled sandwiches and tossed them in the trash.

Over the next hour, there was a sudden influx of customers who seemed to be part of a tourist group. They kept Amy busy. Knowing that he wouldn't have a chance to chat with her again tonight, Joshua decided to leave. He waved at her on the way out, and she acknowledged his departure with a quick smile while she served another customer.

It was dark already, but there were still plenty of people walking around Santa Monica, where the shops on Third Street Promenade were still open. Joshua stopped by a pizza place and ordered a large pizza to take home.

He walked back to his apartment where he devoured half the pizza in front of the TV. But watching TV soon bored him, and after a quick shower, he headed back out. He felt restless. A drive in his car would put him in a better mood. In the past week, he'd gotten rather good at driving, and enjoyed it tremendously. He liked watching people, and many of the bistros and restaurants along Ocean Boulevard and its cross streets had outdoor dining.

Kelly would have liked to dine at a restaurant like that, dressed up in her finest clothes, basking in the admiring gazes of passersby. Joshua shook his head at himself. Kelly had made her choice. He shouldn't even be thinking about her. But the more he watched beautiful women on the arms of handsome men, sitting down to a romantic dinner, the more annoyed he became. Suddenly all gorgeous women he saw looked like Kelly. And all the men looked like him. Yeah, it was time to return to his studio and get a good night's sleep.

When he oriented himself, he realized that he was only a couple of blocks away from the Happy Grind coffee shop, but the place would be closed by now. And even if it wasn't, why would he go back there tonight? To confirm that the computer program used to pair up the time travelers with women of 2025 wasn't infallible and in fact didn't guarantee mutual attraction? To be reminded that Dr. Mandell and Professor Henley had decided to teach him a lesson? Would they have paired him with somebody else, somebody prettier, if he hadn't asked that stupid question during the professor's talk?

Frustrated, Joshua kicked down the gas pedal and, seeing that there was little traffic, he took the next right turn a little faster than usual. A pedestrian running into the street entered his peripheral vision. He stepped on the brake, and swerved so as not to hit the person. And he would have succeeded, had the female pedestrian with the long hair stopped. She bumped against the passenger side of the car, which had finally come to a complete stop.

"Shit!" Joshua yelled, adrenaline pumping through his body. "Fuck!" He spun his head in the direction of the woman, and froze.

"Amy?"

Somewhat dazed, she stared at him. "Joshua?"

"Oh my God! Did I hurt you?" He was about to open the car door to jump out, when Amy looked over her shoulder, then back at him.

"They're chasing me!" Panic was written all over her face.

"Who?" Joshua glanced past her, when he saw a movement half a block away. Two figures were running in Amy's direction.

"The two thieves," she said, breathing hard.

"Jump in, now!" Joshua ordered, glad that he'd left the roof down, because it made it easier for Amy to get in.

The moment she was inside, Joshua stepped on the gas pedal and sped away.

Just in time. A second later, and the two guys would have caught up with them. He made several turns to leave the two would-be attackers in the dust, and kept driving.

"Are you hurt?" He took his eyes off the road for a moment to check for obvious signs of injury. He didn't see any blood.

Amy seemed to shake. "I don't know. I don't think so."

It was evident that she was in shock.

"We'll have a look at you in a minute. Don't worry about anything. You're safe. I'll make sure of it."

But inside, Joshua knew that all this was his fault. He should have known that the two thieves would return to take their anger out on Amy. He should have been there to protect her. She was his responsibility. And he'd make up for it now.

"I promise," he said to Amy and pulled into a parking spot just outside his apartment building.

9

The Dark Knight

When Joshua flipped the light switch and closed the door to his studio behind him and Amy, she seemed to finally come out of her numb state.

She glanced around, arms wrapped around her torso as if she was cold. "You live here?"

He nodded. "It's not much, but I like the area."

"It's very nice."

"Hmm. Take off your jacket," he said and stretched out his hand.

She took a step backward. "Why?"

"So I can see if I hurt you."

"You didn't hurt me."

"I mean when you hit the car. It was quite a bang. It left a dent in the door." He'd seen it when he'd helped her out of the car.

"I'm sorry about your car. I'll pay for it, but I don't have any money right now."

"Amy, I don't care about the car. Besides, it was my fault for coming around the corner so fast. But I'm worried that you're hurt. So, please take off your jacket."

Finally, she nodded and dropped her backpack, which she'd slung over one shoulder, next to the coffee table. Slowly she took off her jacket.

Joshua inspected her front and back, but he couldn't see any blood. "Your backpack must have taken the brunt of the impact. Move your arms up and down."

Amy did as he asked, and he noticed her wince.

"Where does it hurt?"

"I'm fine. It's just a little bruise."

"I'll be the judge of that."

Before she could protest, Joshua had bridged the distance between them with two steps and ran his hands over her ribs. "Does that hurt?"

"No."

He examined her stomach by pressing gently. "How about this?"

"No, it's fine."

He moved his hands to her left hip, when she winced again.

He grunted. "Just like I thought."

"It's not that bad," Amy protested. "It's just a little sore."

"I'll have a look at it."

Amy took a step back. "That's not necessary." Suddenly, her expression became leery.

Did she consider him a sexual predator? He instantly lifted his hands in a show of surrender. "I wasn't trying anything... I mean, that didn't even cross my mind..."

Her eyes darted around the room, taking in her surroundings as if she was looking for a way to escape.

"I'm just..." she started. "After what happened earlier, I'm just a little on edge. It's not you..."

He nodded reassuringly. "What happened when you left the coffee shop?"

"I walked to the bus stop. They were coming toward me... I recognized them immediately. They wanted the money... But I couldn't let them take it. So I ran."

"You're fast," he said.

"I was lucky. I was able to cross the street just before the lights changed and a couple of cars passed. It gave me a head start, but they were catching up. If you hadn't been there... I don't know what they would have done." Amy looked up at him with big eyes. "That's twice now that you've helped me."

For a moment, all he saw were her green eyes. He'd never seen more beautiful eyes in a woman. Their depth seemed endless as if they were truly portals into her soul. He'd always considered that expression trite, but now he understood what was meant by it.

Amy didn't like to accept help from strangers. She didn't want to be a burden. And she wanted nobody's pity. He knew all this just by holding her gaze.

"It's nothing, really." Not wanting to make Amy feel like she owed him something, he changed the subject. "Can I get you something to drink?"

She shook her head, but her gaze strayed past him to the coffee table. He followed her look. He'd forgotten to put the pizza box with the leftover pizza into the refrigerator.

"The pizza is cold," he said.

"But there's some left?"

"Yeah, half of it. It was really too big for me alone." He motioned to the sofa. "Let me get you a plate and some cutlery." He walked to the open-plan kitchen. "Do you want something to drink with it?"

He looked over his shoulder and saw that Amy was already taking a big bite out of one slice.

She stared at him and swallowed quickly. "I'm sorry. I didn't get a chance to eat today."

"Eat, please."

Watching how Amy fairly inhaled one slice after another told him what he was already suspecting: that she didn't always have enough money to eat properly. He made a mental note to take care of that problem.

Joshua poured a glass of sparkling water for Amy and handed her a napkin, before taking a seat next to her on the couch.

"Thank you," she said between bites, then she looked back at the pizza box. One slice remained. He noticed her looking at it, but she didn't take it.

"Finish it," he encouraged her. "I've eaten plenty."

Amy took the last slice and devoured it. Joshua had never seen a girl eat as fast as Amy. Kelly had always picked at her food, never eaten more than a fancy salad or some poached fish for fear of losing her slim figure. Looking at Amy now, he realized that she too was slim, slimmer than she should be, but not by choice.

She took a few sips of the water he'd poured her, before setting down the glass. "Thank you. I should go now."

She made a motion to get up, but Joshua put a hand on her forearm.

"Why don't you just take a break for a minute? Rest. I'll drive you home later."

"I can take the bus."

"And risk those two bastards following you again and attacking you? Not gonna happen."

"But I can take care of myself..." Her voice trailed off.

Joshua looked into her eyes, and saw a wet sheen developing. Amy was on the verge of tears again. What the hell had he done now?

"Amy, I'm sorry," he whispered.

Not knowing what else to do, he pulled her against his chest and wrapped his arms around her in a hug gentle enough so she could withdraw if she wanted to.

"Please let me help you."

10
Let's Get It On

Amy felt Joshua's arms around her, his warmth engulfing her like a protective cocoon. He was the first man who was treating her like a real person with feelings. He was treating her as if she didn't have disfiguring scars, as if she was like any other young woman. She allowed herself to lower the shield she'd built around herself, one that hurtful words and deeds couldn't penetrate.

"Everything will be okay," he murmured

into her hair, while he gently stroked her back to comfort her.

To her surprise, she suddenly felt him press a kiss on top of her head. To know that he wasn't disgusted by her gave her strength. She lifted her head from his chest, bringing her face within inches of his.

"Thank you," she whispered. "Nobody's ever been kind to me like you..."

He didn't pull back, nor did he answer. There was something in his gaze that drew her to him. She didn't know how it happened, whether she made the first move, or whether he did. But their lips met, tentative at first, but neither she nor Joshua pulled back. The touch turned firmer, and she found herself nibbling on his upper lip and licking her tongue over it to taste him. Joshua pulled in a breath of air, and his hand on her back shifted. All of a sudden, one cupped the back of her head, while he tilted his head to one side and captured her lips fully.

Without hesitation, she put her arms around him, one hand on his nape to pull him to her so he wouldn't stop. He tasted good, so male, so wild. She didn't hold back. She loved kissing, but the drunken guys she slept with on occasion were rarely in the mood for kissing. Nor had she ever kissed a man who was sober enough to notice her scarred face, not until now. Joshua's skillful kiss awakened a yearning in her. She wanted to know what it would feel like to make love, not just to fuck in the dark where the guy would barely remember the next day that he'd slept with her.

With parted lips she explored Joshua the way he explored her mouth, while she pressed her breasts against his chest and felt how her nipples hardened in anticipation. The shock from earlier was forgotten, as was the pain in her hip. She wanted... she needed to feel Joshua.

Joshua ripped his lips from hers, his

hands gripping her shoulders to hold her away from him.

"I'm sorry," he said. "I didn't mean to... we shouldn't have... You are..."

His words hit her like an ice-cold shower. Joshua was already regretting having kissed her. She shook off his hands and shrank back. She tightened her jaw. She knew all too well what he was thinking.

"I'm ugly," she said and turned her face so he was forced to see her scarred side.

"That's not what I said," he protested.

She shot up to stand, and he did the same.

"But it's true", she said. "For what it's worth, I got carried away too. I shouldn't have kissed you."

"You didn't. I kissed you."

"What does it matter now? You're disgusted with me. So I'll get out of your hair." She attempted to turn away, but Joshua snatched her arm and stopped her.

"I'm not disgusted."

She glared at him. Her shield was back up. She needed to protect herself from getting hurt. "You don't have to lie to me. No man can stand looking at me." She pointed to her scars, turning her bad side toward him once more. "What man can like this?"

"Your scars have nothing to do with whether you're likeable or desirable," he claimed.

She pressed out a bitter laugh. "It has everything to do with it. As if somebody like you could ever find somebody like me desirable. I'm not that naïve." She was too much of a realist.

"Then you tell me how this happened," he said and jerked her hand toward him and pressed it over the fly of his jeans.

To her utter surprise, she felt a hard ridge there. She tried to pull her hand away, but he put his other hand over it to press it harder onto his erection.

"Tell me," he urged her, his voice beseeching now.

"That's not my fault," Amy said, still defiant.

"Isn't it?" He shook his head. "I don't just get hard-ons for no reason… well, unless it's early morning and I'm just waking up, but that's not the point. The point is that you gave me this hard-on by kissing me."

She felt his cock pulse beneath her palm, and the sensation sent heat through her body. "Then why did you reject me?"

"Reject you?" He shook his head. "I didn't want to steamroll you into doing something you thought you had to do just because you're grateful that I helped you today. You're vulnerable, and I don't take advantage of anybody like that."

She tried to read his eyes to figure out if he could be believed. "I'm not vulnerable."

"That's a lie, and you know it."

He was right, but she wasn't going to admit it, nor did she have an answer to his claim.

"By the way," he suddenly said casually,

his gaze lowering. "How long are you planning on squeezing my cock before you put me out of my misery and open the zipper?"

Her eyes flew to the front of his jeans. Her hand still pressed against the hard ridge of his erection, even though Joshua had removed his hands from hers. As if burned, she jerked back, severing the contact.

When she met his gaze, she found him grinning.

Speechless, she stared at him, when he took a step closer and put his hands on her shoulders.

"So," he murmured, lowering his head to hers. "Do you want to touch my cock? Cause I'd love to feel your hands on me." His breath was hot as he pulled her earlobe between his lips and licked it.

As if they had their own mind, her hands were on his pants a moment later, opening the button, then lowering the zipper.

When she pushed his jeans down to mid-thigh, Joshua whispered in her ear, "Please tell me that you're not doing this because you think you owe me something. 'Cause you don't."

"I've daydreamed about touching you..."

She pulled down his boxer briefs. His cock fell into her hands, and she sighed contentedly. His skin felt like silk. She wrapped her hand around his rock-hard shaft.

Joshua let out a moan. "Fuck!" He placed kisses along her neck, then traveled back to her face, until his lips were hovering over her mouth. "Your hands feel good." He slowly ran his hands down from her shoulders over her torso. "Do you mind?"

When she let out a breathless, "Please," Joshua touched her breasts through her T-shirt and squeezed them gently.

"Lift your arms," he ordered. When she did, he pulled her T-shirt over her head. She wore nothing beneath, and a moment later, his hands were back on her breasts. She shivered at the contact of skin on skin.

"Touch my cock," he said at her lips, then captured them for a deep kiss.

Amy took his cock into her hands and moved them up and down his erection. His size was impressive, but what was even better was his reaction to her caresses. Joshua moaned into her mouth, while he teased her breasts, squeezing them, and turning her nipples into hard little buds.

When he suddenly ripped his lips from hers, Amy worried for a moment that he was going to stop again, but all he did was to take his shirt off and toss it on the floor. Then he reached for the front of her pants and opened the button. But before he could pull down the zipper, Amy gave him a little push so he lost his balance and landed on the sofa.

"What?"

She didn't answer his question, and instead lowered herself to kneel between his legs. She pushed his pants even farther down, and watched him spread his legs wider, his eyes locking with hers.

"Oh God, you're gonna suck me..." he said, amazed.

Holding his gaze, she lowered her head until her lips could touch the tip of his cock. "If you don't want me to, you should stop me now."

"Not a chance," he replied and put his hands on her cheeks.

She flinched. Nobody apart from a doctor or a nurse had ever touched her scarred side. But Joshua kept his hands where they were.

"Just so I can pull out if I get too close," he explained.

She put her lips around the tip of his cock and took his hard shaft as deep as she could.

"Oh fuck!"

11

Love Shack

Joshua cursed when he felt Amy's hot mouth around his hard-on. He'd never felt anything better, and he'd certainly not expected this at all.

Kelly had never given him a blow job. She'd claimed that her gag reflex was too prominent. But he now believed that she wasn't selfless enough to give the man she loved this kind of pleasure. After all, he'd gone down on her, and she'd enjoyed it. She probably considered herself too good to give blow jobs. And clearly, she didn't love him enough to consider his pleasure. Joshua pushed the thoughts about his ex-girlfriend out of his mind, and instead concentrated on Amy.

He had no idea why he'd comforted her one moment, and kissed her the next. Nor did he know why he'd gotten so hard from just a kiss. When Amy had tried to accuse him of stopping because she was ugly—her words, not his—, he'd had to prove that it wasn't the case, even though he knew that her looks had something to do with his hesitation. But the more she'd pushed him away and claimed she didn't want him, the more determined he'd become to prove to her that she turned him on.

And the funny thing was, she did. Her hands on him had fueled a kind of desire in him that he hadn't felt in the last few weeks with Kelly. Was it because Amy was new and a virtual stranger to him? Or was something else at play? Was there more to the algorithm that had matched him up with

Amy? The scientists had claimed that the matching criteria almost guaranteed mutual attraction, though Joshua couldn't quite believe it. It didn't really matter why he was drawn to Amy, but boy, did he enjoy this.

Being imprisoned in Amy's mouth while her hands played with his balls, felt like being engulfed in a cave of heat and wetness. He could barely believe that the woman sucking him with such passion and skill was the same he'd recoiled from when he'd first seen her.

Fuck, no girl had ever sucked him like this. As if Amy enjoyed it as much as he did, which of course was impossible. And with every second, her movements became faster, and her sucking more intense. And the way she scraped her fingers along his tight sac brought him to the brink of an orgasm. But he couldn't allow that. No. When he came, it would be inside Amy's pussy.

Knowing he couldn't last much longer,

Joshua pulled up Amy's head until his cock popped from her lips. With big eyes she met his gaze.

"Don't you like it?" she murmured.

He bent down to kiss her on the lips. "I like it too much."

"Then why did you make me stop?"

He pulled her up onto his lap. "Because I want us to come together."

"Oh."

He caressed her breasts. "So why don't you take off the rest of your clothes?"

She lifted herself off him and started taking off her pants, while he rid himself of his shoes so he could pull off his pants completely. He sat there naked and watched her until she stood before him in only her panties. She lowered her lids as if she was suddenly shy.

"Something wrong?" he asked.

"I don't have any condoms."

He motioned toward the bed. "I do. In the nightstand."

She walked there and he followed her with his eyes. Amy had a perfect figure. A slim waist, slightly cushioned hips, a heart-shaped ass, and perfectly shaped breasts the size of his palms.

When she turned around, she held a condom in her hand.

Joshua crooked his finger and smiled. When she stopped before him, he looked up at her, then slowly slid his fingers underneath her panties and pushed them down her athletic legs to reveal the triangle of dark hair that guarded the entrance to her body.

"Beautiful," he murmured and reached for the condom. He quickly opened the foil packet and slipped the latex over his throbbing cock, anxious to bury himself in Amy's heat.

"Do you like to ride?" he asked and reached for her.

She knew what he wanted, and lowered herself over him, until his cock nudged against her pussy. He placed his hands on her hips and slowly pulled her down onto his cock inch by inch until he was inside her to the hilt.

Amy bit her lip and threw her head back, her breasts thrusting toward him. He didn't pass up the opportunity and licked and sucked her nipples, until she moaned out loud. Farther below, she began to move up and down on him, releasing him, then recapturing him.

Fuck, she was good. She knew when to slow down, when to speed up, when to squeeze him tighter, and when to ease off.

"You know why I love this position?" he asked.

"Why?"

He removed a hand from her hip and brought it to where their bodies were connected. "Because I can do this." He gathered some of Amy's juices, and rubbed his thumb over her clit.

When she gasped, he chuckled. Her hair

fell into her face, and he could barely see the scars now. When he looked at only the unmarred side of her face, he could imagine how she would have looked without the disfiguring scars. She would have been beautiful.

Amy rubbed herself against his thumb, and he noticed how her tempo increased. "You don't mind doing this?"

"This? Touching your clit?" He shook his head. "Am I doing it right?"

Her eyelids fluttered, and her breathing turned more ragged. "Yes.... It's perfect."

She rode him harder and faster, and he could feel that she was getting closer to her own orgasm. He held back, not wanting to come before she did, because for some reason he had the feeling that she needed this more than he did. And he was willing to give her what she needed. Because soon, he would have to tell her what he needed from her.

When Amy's muscles tensed around his

cock, he knew she was close. He doubled his efforts and concentrated only on her, forgetting his own needs. Moments later, she moaned and her interior muscles spasmed around his cock. Instantly, he lost his control and climaxed without warning.

Amy collapsed over him, and Joshua wrapped his arms around her, holding her to him, not ready to leave her body. Like aftershocks, Amy's muscles still contracted around him.

She mumbled something against his shoulder.

"What?" he asked.

"Thank you," she said, this time louder.

"Oh no," he answered, "thank *you*. You were amazing." He ran his hand over her long hair, then pressed a kiss on it. "I hope you're in the mood for more."

She lifted her head, and he was suddenly confronted with her scarred side. Involuntarily, he flinched. The look in her eyes told him that she'd noticed it.

Before she could free herself from his embrace, something she was clearly intending to do, he stroked his fingers over her scars to convince her—and himself—that her scars didn't matter. He wasn't sure how successful his attempt was. "It must have been a terrible accident."

Amy sat back a little and shook her head. "It wasn't an accident."

12
Fatal Attraction

"What happened to you?"

Joshua lay in bed, Amy in his arms, her back turned to him, her tempting ass lining up with his groin. His cock was at rest, but he knew it wouldn't remain at rest. But right now, he wanted to talk. He needed to understand Amy.

"I'm assuming you weren't born with these scars." In fact, he knew it, because he'd seen photos of her when she was just fifteen or sixteen, and her skin had been perfect. But he couldn't tell her that, not yet anyway.

"Why do you want to know?"

"Because I care about you." It was the truth. There was something about Amy that made him want to protect her independent of his mission to bring her back to the future.

"I was in foster care. My parents are drug addicts. I was taken away from them when I was four years old. I spent fourteen years with various different foster families." She sighed. "Nobody wanted to adopt me. I guess I was already past the cute age. I was told that I had a lot of anger in me as a four- and five-year-old."

"That's understandable. I mean, if I had been taken away from my parents at that age, I would have kicked and screamed all day."

"Well, prospective adoptive parents didn't see it that way. They all thought I had behavioral problems." She shrugged. "Maybe I did."

"It wasn't your fault." When she didn't say anything, he pressed a kiss on her shoulder. "Go on."

"I was about to turn sixteen, and I'd only been with my new foster family for a year, when I realized that my foster father was giving me looks that I didn't like."

Joshua's stomach knotted. He could guess where this was leading.

"I was pretty then, you know?"

In fact, he did. He'd seen the photos.

"He wanted me. It started with innocent hugs of encouragement when I was preparing for tests at school. At least I thought they were innocent. But they weren't. With every week, things got worse. His touching became more inappropriate, and I tried to push him away without angering him, but he didn't get the message."

Joshua took her hand and squeezed it.

"I'd met a boy in school. I liked him, and he had a crush on me. We started dating in secret. I couldn't bring him home. But my foster father found out anyway. A neighbor had seen us together, and she told him. She didn't think anything of it, of course. How could she know that my foster father would go berserk?"

She sniffled.

Joshua's heart broke for her. "If you don't want to continue... I understand."

She turned her head to him. "No, I need to continue. I haven't spoken about it in a long time."

He nodded, and she turned away again.

"I didn't know that he knew about my boyfriend. I found out later, far too late. He didn't let on. But I knew something was amiss. He was always in a bad mood, so much so that my foster mother decided to visit her sister for a few days to get a break. I doubt she knew what kind of danger she put me in by leaving for the weekend."

Amy's body seemed to stiffen. "He confronted me as soon as she'd left. He accused me of sleeping around, of being a slut. And he grabbed me. I knew what he wanted to do…"

Joshua's heart began to race. "Did he rape you?"

"He wanted to, but I fought back. I hit him with the first thing I could grab: a half-empty bottle of wine. It only made him angrier. I'd never seen him so furious. That's when he told me that if he couldn't have me then nobody else could either." She sniffled again. "I thought he would kill me, but he was far more brutal. He wanted me to live, but be reminded of him every day."

Joshua turned her in his arms so he could see both sides of her face. Gently, he ran his fingers over her scars. "How did he do it?"

"A frying pan with hot bacon fat." She swallowed hard. "The pain was unbearable. I wanted to die just so I wouldn't feel the pain anymore. When I lay there, screaming and whimpering, he bent over me and said: now nobody will ever desire you again. Every man will find you disgusting, just like you deserve, you little slut."

Joshua pulled her closer to him and stroked her hair to comfort her. He pressed a kiss on her forehead. "I'm so sorry, Amy, so sorry." How could somebody be so cruel, so heartless? "I hope he got what he deserved."

"I told the doctors, and they notified the police. He was charged with aggravated assault. But the trial didn't go my way. The defense claimed that I was lying. The lawyer made everybody believe that I harmed myself. And with my history of behavioral problems documented by social services, the jury believed him, not me. He walked, and I was sent to live in a group home for difficult teenagers until I turned eighteen. Since then, I've been on my own."

How could a jury not have convicted that

bastard? How could they have let him off? What kind of justice was this? It was no justice at all.

"It wasn't fair," Joshua said.

"No, it wasn't."

"And your boyfriend from back then?"

She lifted her head to meet his gaze. "What do you think? He was sixteen and popular at school. He couldn't date a girl like me. Imagine how the rest of the school would have treated him."

"Are you defending him?"

"No. But I understand why he dumped me. It doesn't matter. I got over it."

Maybe, but it couldn't have been easy for her.

"Just like I'll get over it when you stop coming to see me."

Her callous words jolted him. "Why are you saying that?"

"Because it'll happen. You're too good-looking to date somebody like me. And now that you've had me, the novelty will wear off."

"Novelty? I think I'm gonna be offended now," he said and sat up in bed. "What do you think we just did here?"

Amy sat up too, and the sheet dropped to her waist. "We had sex."

Joshua stared at her. He knew what she was doing. She was building a wall around her so she wouldn't get hurt again. She'd shared her story with him, and probably regretted having let him get this close.

"Then I guess I have my work cut out for me."

She gave him a quizzical look. "Doing what?"

"Showing you that..." That he cared about her? No, she wouldn't believe it, he didn't even believe it himself. He didn't understand what he felt for her. Was it pity? Was it the same kind of feeling he had when he came across a wounded animal and nursed it back to health? Perhaps.

"Showing me what?" she asked defiantly. "That you're different from other guys?"

"I am different." How different she would find out soon. "But that's not what I want to show you."

"Then what?"

"I want to show you that you too have something important to contribute to this world. You deserve affection and respect just like anybody else…"

And *love*, but he didn't know whether he would be the one who could give her the love she needed, because he didn't know if he could ever truly look past her external scars. And only somebody who could truly love her for who she was would be able to help her heal her internal scars. Maybe once he'd brought her to the future, there would be somebody who could love her.

Joshua put his hand on her nape and pulled her face to him, while he put his other hand around her back. "So, tell me something. Have you ever slept with the same guy more than once?"

Stunned, her eyes widened. "Why are you—"

"So you haven't. No wonder you think I'm just gonna go away after having sex with you once." He chuckled. "I'm not an only-once kind of guy. You know why?"

"Why?"

"Because it gets better the more often you do it." He moved his hand up her torso to her breasts, caressing the supple flesh. Slowly, he pressed her back onto the mattress. "Now be a good girl and let me take care of you."

13
A Series of
Unfortunate Events

Sunday, April 6, 2025

Amy woke later than usual. It was no surprise. She'd slept well in Joshua's arms. His closeness was comforting and gave her hope that maybe good things were finally happening in her life.

She showered, glad that there was hot water, rather than the cold one she had to put up with at home when several of her roommates had already showered before her. Besides, it was a luxury to have nobody bang on the bathroom door to ask her to hurry up.

By the time she was dressed and ready to leave, Joshua was stirring, but she decided not to kiss him goodbye. Instead, she snuck out before he was fully awake. She didn't want him to see her in the light of day, scars and all. What if he regretted the previous night? It would only rob her of the feeling of happiness that was blooming inside her, because despite all the things he'd said to her, she wasn't sure he meant them. If he did, he knew where she would be: at the coffee shop. And if he came to see her there again, she would be ecstatic, but if he didn't, she would at least have the memory of a beautiful night.

Amy took the bus back to her place and unlocked the door to the apartment building. It was relatively quiet inside, which wasn't unusual for a Sunday morning. After all, most of the students living in the apartments were probably out partying all night and hadn't come home until the early hours of the morning, and were still sleeping.

The elevator was out of order as usual, so she walked up the two flights of stairs. In front of apartment 3F, she stuck her key in the lock. The lock was sticky as so often, but after the second try she managed to unlock the door. She pushed it open, and hit her head against the door. Annoyed she pushed again and lifted her head to look more closely why the door was only opening a few inches. The chain was set from the inside of the apartment.

"Damn it!"

She didn't want to wake her roommates, but she didn't have a choice. One of them had accidentally set the chain without making sure that everybody was at home.

"Hey, anybody awake?" she called out through the gap between door and frame.

There was no answer. Sighing, she tried again, this time louder.

"Hey, it's me, Amy. The chain is on. Can you unlock please?"

This time, she heard a toilet flush. Then the sound of footfalls.

"Hey, it's Amy, let me in," she called out again.

A moment later, the footsteps became louder, and finally, Paula appeared in Amy's field of vision.

"Hey, Amy," she said, frowning.

"Sorry to wake you, but can you please just remove the chain?" How often did she have to ask for it? Wasn't it obvious that she couldn't get in?

"Yeah, about that," Paula started without making any attempt at removing the chain and opening the door fully.

"What's going on?"

"You didn't pay the rent."

"But I was gonna pay this morning," Amy interrupted, feeling panic slither up her spine like a snake. "I've got the money now."

Paula sighed. "It's too late. We voted last night to replace you."

"What?" Dread filled every cell of her body.

"Yeah, you're constantly late with the rent. You're not reliable."

"But you can't just lock me out," Amy protested.

"We can and we did. You're not on the lease. We had another girl move into your room last night. Sorry." Paula shrugged, and it almost looked like she wanted to say something to console her, but then she tipped her chin up. "We packed your things. All your stuff is on the first floor in the corner cupboard next to the mailboxes."

Tears welled up in Amy's eyes, but she tried to push them down. "But what am I gonna do? I have nowhere else to go."

Paula shook her head. "Not our problem. You had enough warnings." Paula leaned in and dropped her voice. "If it had been up to

Tracy, she would have kicked you out a month ago."

Amy held her breath, knowing that if she breathed, she would burst into tears.

"So, please give me your key. If not, we'll change the locks later today."

Knowing she had lost, Amy handed over the keys in almost robotic movements. She was numb now.

She barely noticed when Paula closed the door. She just kept standing there, frozen in disbelief. After the best night of her life, she'd hovered on cloud nine, and a few hours later, she found herself descending into despair. If only she'd gone home last night and paid her rent then, she could have averted this. Instead, she'd allowed herself to enjoy one night of pleasure. One single night. And now she was paying for it. As if she'd asked for too much. Were a few hours of happiness really too much to ask for? Why did she have to pay for the little joy she'd allowed herself to indulge in? And to pay so dearly: She was homeless now. Homeless in a city of millions. What would she do now?

14

In the Midnight Hour

Joshua parked half a block away from the Happy Grind coffee shop. When Amy had gotten up in the morning and taken a shower before leaving, he'd pretended to be asleep. He had no idea how to face her after their unexpected night of passion. He didn't know what it all meant. Yes, the Institute for Time Travel had used a scientific method to select which men were paired with which women from the past to assure maximum compatibility. Did they know something he didn't know? After all, he wasn't attracted to

Amy, yet his body had reacted contrary to his mind. She'd made him harder and hornier than he'd been in a long time.

At first, he'd blamed it on the fact that Amy had looked at him as if he was her hero. What man didn't like basking in the admiring gaze of a grateful woman? And grateful she'd been. More than he'd expected. Her lips around his cock had been out-of-this-world amazing. No wonder he'd fucked her. What man wouldn't? And her body was perfect, maybe a little too thin, but that was something easily changed with the right nutrition, something she would never have to worry about in the future, because every citizen received an allowance that covered their basic needs: food, shelter, healthcare.

He'd loved the feeling of cradling her as she slept in his arms. A protectiveness had come over him when she'd told him how she'd obtained her scars. While he'd made love to her a second time, he hadn't even noticed her scars, but later, when she'd stirred, he'd seen her face in the harsh morning light, and he'd shuddered and chosen the easy way out: to pretend he was still sleeping.

All day, he'd pondered what to do about Amy. Could he in all good conscience take her to the future with him, letting her believe he cared about her, when he had no idea what was going on inside him, how he felt about her?

The odd thing was how his body had behaved after Amy had left his bed. He'd yearned for her to be back in his bed, back in his arms. And at every recollection of their night of sex, he'd gotten aroused all over again.

Still, he'd stopped himself from going to visit her at her flat or at the coffee shop, unsure what to say to her. Because the truth of it was that he loved having sex with her. And that couldn't be right. He was supposed to want a relationship with the woman assigned to him, not just sex. And if Amy found out about his thoughts, surely, she would push him away, not wanting to be used just for sex. He felt like a complete bastard.

All day he'd battled with his conscience, hoping to come up with his next step. One consolation was that they'd given him six months to get to know Amy before he had to make a decision. Maybe after a few months, her scars wouldn't repel him the way they did now. Maybe the attraction would develop eventually. He had to trust in that, or the next few months would be miserable.

Joshua took a deep breath. He felt bad that he hadn't talked to Amy after their night together, and he didn't want her to feel that he'd used her simply for sex. He wanted her to know that he wouldn't dump her unceremoniously. That's why he'd finally driven to the coffee shop. Through the windows, he saw Amy tidying up the shop, and turning the sign on the door from *open* to *closed*.

Any minute now, she'd come out. He would apologize that he hadn't contacted her earlier, and make up some excuse. And after a few kisses, he would drive her home and promise to take her out for a proper date later in the week. Happy with his plan, Joshua stared at the door to the shop. The light inside was switched off, but the door wasn't being opened. From what he knew about the shop, there was no back exit, so why was Amy not coming out?

Joshua waited another three minutes, before he got out of the car, locked it, and walked across the street. At the coffee shop, he tested the door, but it was locked. He pressed his face to the glass to look inside, but he couldn't see Amy from his vantage point. Worried now, he knocked on the glass door.

Finally, he saw a sliver of light inside the shop. It looked like a door to a back room was being opened slightly. Moments later, he recognized Amy. He knocked on the glass again.

"Amy, it's me, Joshua!" he called out, hoping she recognized him despite the burned-out streetlight behind him.

Amy came out from behind the counter and walked to the door, unlocking it. He pulled it open and took a step toward her.

"Joshua," she said, her voice low.

"Hey, Amy, what are you still doing here? Sorry I didn't call or come by earlier," he started, when he ran his eyes over her. His gaze caught on her clothing. She wore a long T-shirt and loose-fitting jogging pants, but only socks, no shoes.

"What are you doing here?" she asked.

"Looking for you, what else?" Then he took a step into the shop and let the door fall shut behind him.

"Oh, ahem," she said, looking embarrassed. "I still have to tidy up here.

Why don't you come by tomorrow? I work the afternoon shift from one till five."

Something wasn't right. He could sense it. Amy was trying to get rid of him—as if she was trying to hide something from him. Or didn't she want to see him anymore after their night of sex? Was he just a one-night-stand for her?

"Hmm." Joshua glanced past her to the door she'd opened. The room was a storeroom, and now, as he focused his eyes on it, he noticed that on the floor lay several of the seat cushions that normally graced the chairs in the coffee shop. It looked like a make-shift bed.

"Ahem, yeah, so, does tomorrow work?" Amy asked, trying to get his attention as she shifted in an obvious attempt to block his view toward the storeroom. But she wasn't tall enough for this. Besides, he already knew what was going on.

"Are you sleeping here?" He hadn't

wanted to sound like he was accusing her, but the words just spilled out.

"Please, Joshua, just go. We can talk tomorrow."

He shook his head. "Tell me what's going on here."

Tears welled up in Amy's eyes. "I lost my room."

Immediately, Joshua pulled her into his arms, feeling the need to comfort her. "How?"

She sniffled. "I was late with my rent. They locked me out."

He stroked his hand over her back. "They can't just do that."

"They can. I'm not on the lease. They gave me five extra days to come up with the money, and I was able to scrape it together." A sob tore from her now. "I was supposed to pay last night, but I didn't get home till this morning, and they'd already given my room to somebody else."

Fuck! In the historical records he'd

studied about Amy, there'd been no note that she'd been thrown out of her shared apartment—because in that timeline she'd never met him. It was clear to him in an instant that it was his fault that she'd been locked out. Had he not made love to her last night, she would have gotten home in time to pay her overdue rent. Instead, she now had to sleep in the storeroom of the coffee shop.

"You can't stay here."

She lifted her head from his chest and stepped out of his embrace. "I have nowhere else to go. Please, don't tell anybody. My boss can't find out, or I'll lose my job too."

Her face was a mask of panic and fear. And desperation. Seeing her like this broke his heart.

"Get your things," he said firmly. "You're staying with me."

After all, he was responsible for her. Not just because he was the reason why she was homeless in the first place, but also because the Institute for Time Travel had made him responsible for Amy by sending him to the past to meet her and convince her to come to 2085 with him. All he was doing was his duty.

"Staying with you?" She stared at him in disbelief. "But you barely know me. You can't just offer me a place to stay."

He had to shake his head at her protest. Amy wasn't used to being given anything she didn't have to work for. That was evident. She took nothing for granted, and he had to admire her for that. Any other woman would have already blamed him for her predicament. Yet Amy was too polite to even mention it, too decent to ask him to make it up to her. And now she didn't even want to accept his offer. Or was she worried, because she didn't really know him? After all, he was practically a stranger to her.

"I know you don't really know me. But I promise I'm not gonna hurt you, Amy. I won't do anything you don't want me to do. This is not a quid pro quo. I don't expect sex in return for this, if that's what you're worried about."

He dropped his gaze to his shoes. What the fuck was he saying? When had he turned into a Good Samaritan? All day he'd thought about having Amy back in his bed, and now he was telling her he didn't expect sex?

With a sigh, he lifted his head and looked straight into her eyes. "Unless you want to, of course. But I would never—"

Amy put her hand on his forearm. "I know." For the first time this evening, she smiled. "Why are you so nice to me?"

He smiled back at her. "Because you need it." Then he pointed to the storeroom. "Shall we get your things? I've got the car outside."

15

We'll Share the Shelter

Amy had to pinch herself when she entered Joshua's studio apartment. Was she asleep in the coffee shop, dreaming all this? Or had Joshua really swooped in and rescued her again?

She felt like she was in a trance when Joshua helped her with her bags and made space for her things in his closet—which to her surprise only contained a few items. She declined his offer of food, because she'd been able to eat leftovers at the coffee shop. But when he asked her if she wanted to take a bath to relax, she nodded, mainly because she needed time to digest what was happening.

As she lay in the bathtub, the hot water soothing her tired bones and her aching feet, she closed her eyes for a few minutes. This was real. Joshua had offered his help without hesitation, even though he didn't have to. Just because they'd had sex the night before, didn't obligate him to suddenly offer her a place to stay. So what exactly was his reason for doing this? More sex? A man looking like Joshua could get sex anytime he wanted without having to offer a girl a place to stay. Then why?

No matter how long and how hard she thought about it, she couldn't figure out why he was doing this for her. But she wasn't going to look a gift horse in the mouth. At least not tonight. Tomorrow, after a good night's sleep, she would figure something out, find something more permanent—because she had no illusions about Joshua: sooner or later, he'd grow tired of her, just as soon as he realized that he could do better than her.

But in the meantime, she'd allow herself to make a few good memories.

Amy stepped out of the tub and pulled the plug to drain it. She reached for a towel and dried herself, then wrapped it around her torso and looked in the mirror. When she tilted her head and combed her hair just right, she could almost hide the ugly side of her face. In the mirror, the girl staring back at her was the Amy before the assault, the girl who'd had dreams, the girl who'd been pretty. It seemed like a lifetime ago.

With a sigh, she turned away from the mirror and opened the door. She stepped into the main room of the studio, where one side was furnished as a living/dining room, the other as a bedroom.

Joshua sat on the sofa, dressed only in

a pair of jeans, his chest bare, his skin glistening as if he was perspiring even though it wasn't overly hot in the apartment.

He turned his head and ran his eyes over her, making her hesitate. Slowly, he rose and took a couple of steps toward her.

"Did the bath help you relax a bit?"

Amy nodded. "Thank you. It was just what I needed." Barefoot, she approached.

"I hope you don't mind, but we should probably share the bed." He motioned to the sofa. "The couch isn't very comfortable to sleep on."

"Of course, I don't mind." She cast a stolen look at his chest, admiring his toned abs and the smoothness of his skin. The sight tempted her, made her yearn for his touch.

"Do you mind if I..." She hesitated, not knowing if she had the courage to be bold.

"If you what?" Joshua asked softly, one hand on the button of his jeans now.

She swallowed away her shyness. "If I sleep in the nude?"

Was it an optical illusion, or did his jeans suddenly appear to stretch more tightly over his groin?

When he didn't say anything, she lifted her gaze to his face and saw him grin. "Only if I may sleep in the nude too."

Encouraged by his response, she stepped closer. "Fair is fair."

He popped the button of his pants open and lowered the zipper. Then he stopped. "Why don't you hang that towel over the chair and get into bed?"

Slowly, Amy released the towel where she'd tucked it in, and pulled it off her, before she draped it over the chair so it could dry overnight. When she looked back at Joshua, she noticed him run his eyes over her, his gaze hungry, his lips parted, while he rid himself of his pants.

Amy lifted the duvet and pulled it aside, then laid down on the mattress without covering herself with the duvet, while she continued looking at Joshua. He was already freeing himself of his boxer briefs, revealing his hard-on. His cock was just as hard and thick as she remembered from the night before. Instinctively, she licked her lips.

With a chuckle, Joshua approached the bed. "Oh no, you're not gonna suck me tonight." He joined her on the bed. "Or I won't last long."

Joshua pulled her into his arms, his face only inches from hers, their chests touching, their legs brushing against one another.

"I hope I'm reading the signs correctly that you want me to make love to you... I figured since you wanted to sleep in the nude..."

Amy put her finger over his lips. "You're very good at reading signs."

He smirked. "I'm even better at other things."

"Anybody could say that." She put her

hand on his nape, pulling him closer. "How about you show me what you're good at?"

"I thought you'd never ask." Joshua captured her lips and kissed her.

Joshua rolled over Amy, while he kissed her deeply. Damn, he'd missed feeling her body molding to his, her lips yielding to his demand for a passionate exchange. At first, when he'd brought Amy back to his apartment and had seen her face in the harsh light once more, he'd actually contemplated sleeping on the sofa. But the moment she'd stepped out of the bathroom, everything male inside him had overridden his perception of outward beauty. Instead, his sex drive had taken over, and he'd seen only one thing: a young woman who welcomed his touch. Instantly, his cock had turned as hard as an iron flagpole. There was no turning back now. All he could think of was making love to Amy, no matter the consequences.

Amy's lips were soft, and her tongue responded to him with languid strokes. He felt her hands on him, one on his nape, pulling him closer, the other on his butt, stroking him. Just like the previous night, she wasn't shy at showing him what she wanted from him. She didn't toy with him, didn't pretend, didn't tease like other girls. She was straightforward, not hiding that he excited her, a fact he deduced from her moans of pleasure and the gentle rocking of her pelvis against his.

The soft glow of the bedside lamp, the only light source now illuminating his apartment, bathed them in a romantic glow. Joshua brushed one hand over her breast and noticed that her nipple was hard. Loving the feel of it, he squeezed the round globe in his hand, the nipple rubbing against his palm. The contact sent a shiver down his spine and made his cock twitch in anticipation.

Amy molded her body to his, asking for more caresses, and he was only too happy to comply. He didn't want to think about where things would go from here, how he would proceed tomorrow, because right now he didn't want to make decisions. All he wanted was to find pleasure with the woman in his arms, and give her the same pleasure in return.

Slowly, Joshua released her lips and lowered his face to her breasts. He licked over one hard nipple, before sucking it into his mouth, while he kneaded the other one in his palm. Below him, Amy arched her back, silently asking for more. He sucked her nipple into his mouth, loving the strangled moan that rolled over Amy's lips in response. He smiled against her skin and lifted his head by an inch.

"Easy, baby, I'll give you what you need."

Because he knew what she needed right

now: to forget the troubles of her life and let herself fall.

"Joshua, let me feel you inside me," she begged.

And even though he knew he should extend their foreplay, he couldn't resist her siren call.

"Anything you want," he murmured and reached for the bedside table.

From the drawer, he retrieved a condom and rolled it over his erection. Then he turned back to her, and noticed Amy's eyes shine with lust and passion. The green of her eyes was even more vibrant than the previous night, even more beautiful. He realized then that it was her eyes that drew him to her and made her marred skin melt into the background, out of focus, forgotten.

Amy spread her legs wider, and without hesitation, he accepted the space she'd made for him. He adjusted himself, then drove his cock deep into her, seating himself to the hilt. Warmth and wetness greeted him.

Amy gasped. "Oh!"

"You all right? Too fast?"

"No, perfect. Just like the rest of you."

His chest filled with pride at the knowledge that the woman in his arms approved of him wholeheartedly.

"Good." He pulled out halfway, then plunged back in and found his rhythm.

Amy moved with him, her hands gripping his hips tightly now, as if she was afraid that he'd stop.

He dipped his head to hers. "I love being inside you."

He didn't give her a chance to reply. Instead, he captured her lips again and kissed her deeply. He poured every ounce of passion into the kiss, while his body moved in sync with Amy's, separating and coming back together in such perfect rhythm that to an outsider it would have looked as if they'd done this a million times before. But he was only just getting to know Amy's body, and he registered every clue her responses gave him to adjust his movements to her needs.

He tightened the leash with which he held on to his self-control, because he didn't want to come before her. But he knew enough about women to know that it wasn't always easy for a woman to find release. Maybe this position wasn't quite right for her.

Joshua pulled out of her.

Panicked, Amy stared at him. "Joshua?"

"Get on your hands and knees, baby," he ordered.

The panicked look on her face vanished, and she turned around and got on her hands and knees. Joshua got behind her and gripped her hips, then drove deep into her.

"Oh, that's good." Amy released a deep sigh.

"I can make it even better," he promised and released one hip.

He brought his hand to her front and combed his fingers through her pubic hair, while he continued to thrust evenly from behind.

"Tell me how you want me to caress your clit."

There was a short hesitation, but then she took his hand and directed it to her center of pleasure. She took his middle finger and pressed it onto her clitoris, then moved it in a circular rhythm.

"Like this," she murmured, before she let go of his hand and braced herself on the mattress again.

"Good."

He continued to caress her clitoris with gentle circular motions, her plentiful juices making the action smooth. At the same time, he eased up on his thrusts with his cock, rocking only gently an inch forward and an inch back to allow Amy to concentrate on her own pleasure.

It didn't take long until Amy's breathing

changed, and her pelvis rocked in a faster tempo, making him speed up his movements on her clit too, while he plunged deeper and harder into her.

"Oh, God, I, I..." She moaned out loud, and a moment later, he felt her pussy spasm and squeeze his cock even tighter than before.

Without warning, he climaxed. He had to hold onto Amy's hips for balance, his body trembling with the sensations of his orgasm.

When Amy's spasms finally subsided, Joshua pulled out of her and rid himself of the condom, before he joined her back on the bed.

He pulled her into his arms. "That was..." He let out a breath, not finding the words for what he wanted to say. "...just wow."

Amy snuggled against him, her face buried in the crook of his neck, one thigh draped over his body, one hand on his chest.

"You're an amazing lover, Joshua."

"It's easy with you." Because for some

reason he didn't feel like he had to perform, or live up to somebody else's expectations. He could just be himself. Maybe that's why sex with Amy was so fulfilling. "You feel so good." He put his hand on her ass and pulled her closer. "How much sleep do you need?"

"Not much."

"Good, 'cause I'm just getting warmed up."

16
We've Gotta Get Out of This Place

Monday, April 7, 2025

Despite making love to Amy long into the night, Joshua woke early, yet remained in bed with her while she continued sleeping. He had to think about what to do next. The fact that Amy had lost her room meant that things were moving faster than he'd expected. Considering her financial situation, chances were that Amy would have a hard time finding new accommodations. She would have to stay with him. And while he certainly enjoyed the physical benefits of that arrangement, he wasn't ready to commit to a long-term relationship with her. And he didn't want to lead her on either. It wasn't fair.

The more he thought about it, the more it became clear that it was best to tell her about the future now, and convince her to come to 2085 with him sooner rather than wait until his six months in 2025 were up. In 2085 she would have a chance at a carefree life, without financial worries to cloud her judgment. And if, once back in the future, he still felt sexually drawn to her, and she to him, maybe they could take this a step further. However, if they weren't meant to have a lasting relationship, at least Amy would be alive and not die in the upcoming pandemic that would wipe out over 50 million people worldwide. And there would be plenty of young men in 2085, men who weren't time traveling back to 2025, who were looking for a wife who could bear children.

Even though he knew now what he had to do, he hated himself for his doubts about Amy. At least with himself he could be honest: if Amy didn't have disfiguring scars, he would so easily fall in love with her. After all, she was sweet, caring, and amazing in bed. He loved the way she felt in his arms, and he felt protective toward her. But it was hard to look past her face. He knew it meant he was shallow and a jerk for thinking like this. However, all his previous girlfriends had been beautiful, stunning even, and right now, he couldn't see himself introducing Amy to his friends and family. Would they talk about them behind his back? Would they make fun of her, and him in the same breath? Could he live with that?

Fuck! He wished he didn't have these thoughts. But maybe the first step to overcoming these obstacles was to acknowledge that they existed.

Feeling a little better about the situation he was in, Joshua got out of bed as quietly as possible and took a shower. When he was done and getting dressed, he heard Amy stir and looked over his shoulder to the bed.

She lifted her head. "What time is it?"

"Early." He slipped into his shirt and started to button it. "I'll go get us some breakfast. Don't go anywhere. I'll be back in twenty minutes."

She sat up, and the sheet slipped down to her waist, exposing her naked breasts. Instantly, something inside him stirred, and he recognized it as lust.

He ripped his gaze from her beautiful curves and looked into her eyes. "I'll try to be back in fifteen."

A soft smile formed around her lips, and she looked almost beautiful.

He had to force himself to walk toward the door instead of the bed, and left the apartment.

The coffee shop around the corner was busier than expected, and it took him twenty-five minutes before he entered his studio again, two cups of fancy coffee and a bag of pastries in his hands. While the door fell shut behind him, his gaze drifted to the bed, but it was empty. For a moment, shock charged through him, but then he heard sounds coming from the bathroom, and he began to relax. Amy was still here. He wasn't entirely sure why that fact filled him with joy, but it did. He was starting to care about Amy—like he cared about a good friend. Well, a friend with whom he had sex.

By the time Amy came out of the bathroom, now dressed in a pair of jeans and a tank top, her hair still wet from her shower, he'd cleared the coffee table and set the coffee cups and pastries down on it.

"Thank you for getting breakfast."

She smiled at him and sat down next to him on the couch. He leaned toward her and kissed her gently on the lips, before he reached for his coffee and settled back in the cushions.

It was time to tell her the truth about why they'd met and who he really was.

"There's something I need to tell you," Joshua started, suddenly feeling nervous about what was ahead of him.

Amy almost choked on her first sip of the latte that Joshua had brought for her. She noticed his serious facial expression, and her heart sank. He probably regretted now that he'd offered her to stay at his place, having acted in the spur of the moment, and was looking for a way to get her to leave. She should have known that her luck wouldn't last.

Steeling herself, she set her cup back on the coffee table. "Yes?"

To her surprise, Joshua took her hands into his and turned his body toward her to face her directly. "I haven't told you much about me, and there's a reason for that. But with all that's happened since we met, and with you having lost your room because of me—"

"It wasn't your fault," she protested automatically.

But he shook his head and smiled at her. "No, it's my fault. But that's not what I need to talk to you about. It's about where I'm from. Or rather when."

Her forehead furrowed. "What do you mean?"

He took a visible breath. "Now, this might sound fantastic, but it's the truth. I'm from 2085, and I've traveled back in time to save you from a pandemic and take you back to the future with me."

All air rushed out of her lungs and she freed her hands from his, while she moved back on the sofa. Already, she was shaking her head. Disappointment rushed through her. How cruel of him. She would have never pegged him to be so heartless, but to come up with such a cruel prank, could only mean one thing.

"You went through my sketchbook. You saw what I'm drawing. How could you?" She jumped up.

Joshua rose from the sofa and stared at her as if she'd gone crazy. "What sketchbook? Listen, I don't know what you're talking about. But you have to believe me: I'm from the future, and I'm here to take you back with me so you won't die in the pandemic."

"Drop it, Joshua." Tears threatened to cut off her airways, but she forced them down and looked around the studio. She spotted her backpack. "I don't need you making fun of me."

"I'm not making fun of you, Amy. I would never."

She glared at him. "Wouldn't you?" She reached for her backpack and pulled out her sketchbook. She opened it and turned back to him, showing it to him. "You saw this, didn't you? You went through my stuff while I was sleeping."

He stared first at her, then at the sketchbook. His facial expression changed to one of surprise, and he reached for the sketchbook. "You drew these?"

She didn't respond. Instead, she pressed her lips together, trying to hold back the sobs. Joshua paged through the sketchbook, his face showing true surprise and interest. The drawings depicted scenes from a different world, a future world, one that she'd dreamed up to escape from this one for a while. A world where life was easier, one where she wouldn't have to struggle every day just to be able to eat and have a roof over her head.

Joshua lifted his head and looked straight at her. "These are amazing. You're an artist. A very talented one. And your imagination..." He shook his head. "It's as if you've already seen glimpses of the future I come from."

A sob tore from her chest. "Please just stop with the charade. I'm packing my things, and I'll leave."

Joshua laid the sketchbook on the coffee table. "Don't, Amy. It's not a charade. I can prove to you that I'm from the future." He shoved the sleeve of his shirt back to his elbow and tapped on his left wrist.

She was about to turn away, when she saw a hologram appear. It hovered over Joshua's arm and moved with him when he moved closer to her. Instinctively, she took a step back, but she couldn't tear her eyes away from the mirage. She'd watched sci-fi shows on television and was familiar with holograms, but she knew that they didn't really exist outside of a movie studio. For certain, no person could project a hologram from his or her naked wrist. Because there was no electronic device on Joshua's wrist that could have conjured up such a thing.

Amy wasn't sure she knew how long

she'd stared at the hologram, when Joshua finally spoke again.

"It's called a holocom. In my time, everybody over the age of five has one on their wrist. It carries all our information, our medical history... it does everything a smartphone does, and so much more."

"But there's nothing on your wrist," she protested, still skeptical. "Is it implanted?"

He shook his head and grabbed his left wrist. The hologram disappeared, and he turned the palm of his right hand to her. In it lay a rigid gold-colored bracelet not wider than an inch. She stared at it in disbelief, then looked back at his wrist.

"But your skin is much darker than this... this holocom." So why hadn't she noticed this on his wrist before?

"That's because it changes its color and texture to whatever my skin looks like. When my skin gets darker because I spend more time in the sun, the holocom changes with it."

He put the holocom back on his wrist, and before her eyes, it adjusted to Joshua's skin, and she couldn't make it out anymore. As if it was invisible. She put her hand on it, but she couldn't even feel a difference between Joshua's skin and the holocom. She tapped on it, but the hologram didn't pop up like it had before when he'd done it.

"It's not working anymore."

"It's genetically encoded. Only my touch can activate it." He tapped on his wrist once again, and the hologram popped up and hovered above his arm. "Will you let me tell you everything now?"

She nodded. She would listen to him, even though his claim was outlandish, but the electronic device on his arm intrigued her.

"Sit to my right so you can see the hologram better, and I'll show you things while I tell you why I'm here."

Joshua sat back down on the couch, and Amy took a seat next to him. He tapped on the images that hovered over his arm, and Amy realized that it looked very much like a computer screen, with icons for different programs.

"Let's start with what brought me here," he started and pointed to various headlines that spoke of a pandemic. "In the fall and winter of 2025, a virus will spread rapidly around the world. At first, the scientists thought it was just a bad form of a flu strain, but it was much worse. Over fifty million people died worldwide."

Amy shrugged. "The flu kills vulnerable people every year. That's nothing new."

"But it wasn't just a flu." He tapped on another area of the holocom and a medical graphic appeared together with another headline. *2025 virus caused gene mutation leading to infertility in females.*

Joshua looked at her. "In my time, ninety-nine percent of all women are infertile, because those women who were infected by the virus in 2025, but survived it, passed a mutated gene on to their offspring. By the time the geneticists figured out what had happened, it was already too late. Birthrates are practically at zero. The human race is going extinct."

The claim sounded unbelievable, but the news reports and articles Joshua pulled up on his holocom, many of them dated in the 2070s and 2080s looked genuine. However, she knew that anything on the internet could be faked. "So you're saying humans in the future are infertile and will die out?"

"Not all humans are infertile. Only women. The men don't have the gene mutation. I can father children, but there are so few women left to repopulate the planet that the world governments came up with a solution: to bring women back from before the 2025 virus could infect them."

She'd read enough sci-fi and time travel novels to know that there was a fundamental flaw in Joshua's story. "But you can't do that. If you take women out of this time and transplant them into yours—that is *if* you're really from the future—then you're changing the future, because—"

He lifted his hand. "I know, we would alter the past, which would alter the future I'm from, but that won't be the case if we take women to 2085 who would have died during the pandemic, and therefore wouldn't have had any significant effect on this timeline."

Amy's breath caught when she realized what this meant. "Are you saying... are you saying that..." She shook her head. She couldn't even say the words.

"I'm sorry." He tapped on something on the holocom, and several documents opened. "You'll be infected in early October this year, and will die a week later."

Amy stared at the death certificate that carried her name. Joshua swiped over the document and revealed a newspaper article that listed names of Los Angeles residents who'd died of the virus in the first two weeks of October 2025. When he zoomed in, one name caught her attention: her own.

"No." She shook her head. "No. That can't be."

Joshua put his hand on her arm and squeezed it. "But you don't have to die. Come to the future with me and you'll have a long life, one where you'll want for nothing. You'll never have to worry about where your next meal will come from, or whether you have a place to stay. Everything will be taken care of for you."

It sounded too good to be true. "This must be a mistake. Please tell me you're joking. Tell me you're playing a prank." But one look into his eyes, and she knew he wasn't lying to her.

She sniffled, her head spinning. But she needed to know more, needed to understand what she was getting herself into. "And you? How many women do you have to bring back?"

"Just one: you."

"Why? You'll need hundreds of thousands of women if you want to raise the birthrate."

"That's why I'm not the only one who travelled to the past. There are tens of thousands of young men like myself who're taking this trip back all over the world. And the program is only just beginning. If it's successful, more men will be sent back."

She drew in a long breath, still trying to wrap her head around it all. "And you chose me?" She turned her face so he had to look at her scars. "Why me?" She gestured to his face. "You could do better than me."

Joshua took her hands and pulled her to him. "Don't say that." He hesitated.

There was something in his eyes that looked like he was hiding something from her. She pulled back a little. "You didn't choose me, did you? Somebody else did."

The moment she said the words, she saw in his eyes that she was right.

Joshua nodded, looking somewhat

embarrassed. "We were chosen for each other because our genetics and personalities provide the best chance of being an ideal match. Not just to produce children, but also to…" Again, he hesitated. "To fall in love."

"I understand." It was sobering to hear that it had all been initiated by somebody other than Joshua. "Did they force you to do this?"

"They? You mean the Institute for Time Travel? No, of course not. I volunteered. Just like all the other guys."

"But you didn't get to choose which woman to bring back, did you?"

He sighed. "That's true. But you and I, we have chemistry. You can't deny that." He took her chin with his thumb and forefinger and brought his lips close to hers. "In fact, I believe we set the bedsheets on fire last night."

She had to smile. "I guess we did."

He kissed her gently, before releasing her again.

"So when are you supposed to take me back to the future?"

"Before September 29th. But given that there isn't anything holding you here, we can go earlier. Tonight, tomorrow, at the end of this week. Next month. Whenever you're ready."

It was sudden, but Joshua was right. She didn't have anything to hold her here. But she had to find out more about the future first, before she could leave the past behind her.

"Tell me more about the future," she demanded.

17

A Farewell to Friends

For hours, Amy asked questions, and Joshua answered them. The more he told her about the future, the more she was certain that he wasn't lying. His answers remained consistent, no matter how often she asked. The things he showed her on his holocom, pictures of the future, newspaper articles and government records of events still to come, helped her believe in his words. Nobody would go through so much trouble to set up such an elaborate prank. The technology of the holocom alone was far too advanced for a college-aged guy like Joshua to own. Maybe a tech billionaire could somehow get a fancy prototype like this made, but even then, she doubted that it would work like Joshua's holocom worked.

"How does it change its color and texture to adapt to your skin?" Amy asked.

"There's a technology that was developed from the stem cells of chameleons. Just like they adapt to their environments, so does the holocom. If you come to the future with me, they'll fit you with one too."

"What else is it used for other than like the internet?"

"You can make payments with it, because it's connected to your funds. And any doctor can access your medical history in case of—"

"Funds?" she interrupted. "But I have no money."

"Every citizen of the world receives a basic amount that covers things like food and shelter. Healthcare is free, so you'll never have to worry about that."

She was surprised at that. Why would a government be so generous? "Does that mean people don't work anymore?"

"No, they work, but in jobs they enjoy. Many of the menial and back-breaking jobs are automated. By giving people enough money to take care of their survival, they've been given the freedom to educate themselves, work in jobs that fulfill them, and have enough time for enjoyment, self-fulfillment, and innovation."

"Self-fulfillment and innovation?"

Joshua nodded toward her sketchbook. "You could devote your time to your art, learn everything you want to learn, and be an artist if you want."

The freedom this thought awakened in her, was indescribable. What would it be like to not have to worry about survival anymore? "It sounds like heaven."

He chuckled. "Don't get me wrong. Not

everything in the future is perfect. The worry for our species' existence has put a damper on things. The population is aging, which brings a lot of problems with it. Life experiences aren't passed down to the next generation anymore, because there barely is a next generation."

"I understand that." And she knew what she had to do to change that. "If I come with you, I'll have a duty to perform, won't I?"

He nodded. "Yes. You'll be expected to bear children."

Images of *The Handmaid's Tale* suddenly popped into her head. What if it was like that? What if she would simply be a broodmare?

"There's something I need to know."

"Ask."

She took a deep breath. "Will I be passed around to different men, so everybody gets a chance at having a child?" The thought made her shudder.

Joshua jerked back, shock on his face. He quickly shook his head. "No! Of course not! When it comes to relationships and marriages, 2085 is still very much the same as 2025. You'll be with the person you love. And nobody expects you to pop out a baby every year. No. That's not what this is about. Yes, the Institute for Time Travel hopes that the women from 2025 will bear at least two children, hopefully three or four, to give civilization the boost it needs. But it's still your choice, and that of your partner."

"Oh." Relief flooded her.

"And there are still divorces. Couples still cheat on each other. But there are also happy marriages. My parents have a wonderful relationship. And nobody cares anymore about the color of your skin."

"You mean there's no more racism?" That astonished her.

"No. There were race riots in the early 2030s. After that, the nations of the world got together to eradicate the economic inequalities everywhere. Once those were dealt with, and everybody enjoyed the same standard of living, race didn't matter anymore. Because it was never really about race, even in your time. It was always about the scarcity of resources and jobs, about financial and economic inequalities. Remove those, and you remove racism."

"That easy?"

"It was never easy. It took decades; it took wars to get there. We only achieved it around the time I was born, in 2063."

"It's so much to take in."

"I know it is. And I wouldn't have sprung this on you so early, but why work yourself to the bone here and constantly worry about everything, when you have a better option? Think about it."

She nodded. "I will."

"All right. In the meantime, how about I get us some takeout?"

Amy nodded. "That sounds great."

Joshua snatched his keys. "How does

Thai sound? I found this great place on Montana."

"I'd love that."

Moments later, Joshua was gone, and she was alone with her thoughts. She looked at her meager possessions. Was there anything worth taking to the future with her if she indeed decided to go? She reached for the sketchpad. It was the only thing she wouldn't want to leave behind. When she dug for her wallet in her backpack, her fingers wrapped around a set of keys. She pulled it out.

Crap! She still had Mr. Mercola's keys for the coffee shop. She hadn't seen him since the day when he'd asked her to lock up at night. She should return them, and though she had never liked him much, at least returning to the coffee shop meant she could say goodbye to Rosie.

She scribbled a quick note for Joshua, before she left fand let the door fall shut behind her. In the hallway she suddenly realized that she'd already made her decision. She would travel to the future with Joshua.

It was only a short walk from Joshua's apartment to the coffee shop. Before entering she glanced through the windows to make sure Mr. Mercola wasn't around. It was late afternoon, and only a few patrons sat at the tables. Amy entered and heard the door chime to announce her arrival.

Rosie looked up and met her gaze. "Amy!" She lowered her voice and motioned her to approach. "Where the hell have you been? Mr. Mercola is gonna be here in about twenty minutes, and if you're not working, he's gonna flip. I've been covering for you."

Amy felt her heart warm. Rosie had been the only person who'd ever been nice to her. "I've just come to return his keys." She laid the keys on the counter. "And to say goodbye to you."

"Goodbye? What? Why? Where are you going?"

"I met someone." She smiled at Rosie. "He's taking me away from here."

"But, Amy, who is he? When did you meet him?" The words were fairly tumbling over her lips, and she saw the concern in Rosie's face. Amy felt the need to alleviate her concerns.

"You won't believe me if I tell you."

"Now you're making me worried."

Amy sighed. She knew that she wasn't supposed to tell anybody about the future. But there had to be exceptions, right? And she would only tell Rosie what she needed to know.

"You can never tell anybody what I'm gonna tell you now. Promise."

"Promise," Rosie said and leaned in.

18
Brave New World

"Ready?"

Amy nodded and put her arms around Joshua. They stood in the middle of the Los Angeles National Cemetery near the UCLA campus. It was close to midnight, and they were the only people far and wide.

"Couldn't we have just traveled back in time from your apartment?" Amy asked, feeling a little creeped out about the graves around them.

"I'm afraid not. The flat I rented doesn't exist in 2085. It's now in the ocean. But this cemetery is where the Institute for Time Travel is located. We're only traveling through time, not through space."

She nodded, more nervous now than when she'd made the decision to go with Joshua. "Okay. I'm ready."

While she had her arms wrapped around Joshua, he pressed a button on his black watch. She wore a similar one, but hers was silver. A split second later, the night around them changed, became blurred. Everything was out of focus and suddenly began to spin around them. Pixels formed and turned into different colors. It wasn't night anymore. But it wasn't day either. As if everything was dissolving and then reassembling around them. The only constant was Joshua, whose arms were now around her, holding her close.

She was blinded by a sudden whiteness around them, but out of the white, colors emerged, and pixels were drawn to each other as if pulled by a strong magnet.

Around them, a new world formed, until everything turned into focus again.

"We're here," Joshua said.

Saturday, July 21, 2085

The Institute for Time Travel wasn't at all what Amy had expected. Not that she knew what she'd really expected, but, at least not this. They were standing in a large hall that reminded her of an indoor sports arena. It was divided into different sections, which were labeled with large signs. Men and women dressed in white full-body hazmat suits were busy attending to young couples and leading them to different, cordoned-off areas that reminded her of the treatment areas in the emergency room of a large hospital.

Joshua released her from his embrace and looked around.

A woman in a hazmat suit approached them. Her mouth and nose were hidden behind a surgical mask. A hologram—projected from her holocom—was hovering over her arm. "Identify yourself, please."

Joshua tapped on his arm, and his holocom opened.

A beep sounded, and the woman nodded. "Welcome back, Joshua Fletcher, Romeo number 48." Then she swept her gaze over Amy, startled for a brief moment, before she looked at the hologram again, clearly comparing her to a picture in her records. A picture that presumably didn't show Amy's scars. "Oh, you must be Amy Brooks. Welcome to 2085." Then she added, "Please hand me your time-travel watches."

Amy removed the silver watch Joshua had given her to time travel, and Joshua did the same and handed both to the woman.

The woman pointed to a sign that said *New Arrivals 1 – 50*. "Please line up behind this sign. You're number 48 and will undergo a medical examination before you'll be led to your quarantine quarters."

"Quarantine?" Amy asked and glanced at Joshua.

He furrowed his forehead. "I wasn't aware we'd be quarantined," Joshua said, addressing the woman.

"I'm afraid it's necessary. A few hours ago, we had an arrival, who showed symptoms of an infectious disease from 2025, and are therefore taking precautions."

"Not the virus," Amy said, scared all of a sudden. What were the odds of having escaped the pandemic, only to get sick here in 2085?

The woman turned to her, and even though her mouth wasn't visible, Amy recognized that she was smiling. "Nothing of the sort. We're just being overly cautious. You'll undergo a quick full-body scan, and there'll be a blood draw. Once the results come back negative, quarantine will be lifted."

"Thank you, ma'am," Joshua said and

took Amy's hand. "Come. Let's take care of this."

Amy allowed Joshua to lead her to the indicated sign. He cast her an encouraging look. "Don't look so worried. It'll all be fine."

As they walked to the indicated sign, Amy looked around. Other young couples like them were standing in lines or walking from one area to the next. It was all very orderly—and very sterile. Images of sci-fi movies where people were controlled by machines came to mind. What if she was marching to her doom?

When they arrived at the sign that said *New Arrivals 1 – 50*, a man dressed in scrubs and a surgical mask greeted them and ushered them behind a curtain. He looked at Joshua and pointed to a large machine that looked like the security check used at airports.

"Please scan your global ID number," the man ordered.

Joshua tapped on his holocom and held

it over the scanner at the machine's entrance. Again, there was a beep. This time, Joshua's photo appeared on the screen next to the scanner. Then Amy saw an old photo of herself appear next to his: a photo that was taken before she'd sustained her disfiguring injury.

"Joshua Fletcher, please step into the scanner," the man said.

It took only a few seconds, before Joshua was done, and left the machine again.

"Now your guest from 2025," he said and looked at the name below Amy's picture. He glanced back at her. "I guess this picture is from a while ago." He pointed to the scanner. "Please step inside."

Amy followed his instructions. When she exited the machine, the man was already pressing a cylinder the diameter of a shot glass onto the inside of Joshua's elbow. A moment later, there was a hissing sound, then the man removed the item and slid it into a machine, where it disappeared. He tapped on a virtual keyboard, before a hologram with the message *Blood sample for Joshua Fletcher accepted* popped up.

She barely had time to take in the technology she was faced with, and realize how automated everything seemed to be, when the man pressed a fresh cylinder onto her arm. She felt a sting, and gasped in shock, but the pain was only temporary. Moments later, her blood sample was accepted by the machine.

"That's it. The results will be available in approximately twenty-four hours. During this time, you'll both be staying together in a self-contained pod. Please follow the signs to *Pods 1 – 50* at the end of this corridor." The man pushed the curtain aside, and revealed a corridor. "An assistant will meet you there to explain everything."

Amy nodded numbly. "Thank you." This looked more and more like they were lab rats that were being led to the slaughter. A cold shiver ran down her spine. Had she made the biggest mistake of her life by trusting Joshua?

At the end of the corridor, a woman dressed like a nurse was expecting them.

"Romeo 48?" she asked with a smile.

This time, Amy could see her smile, because this woman wore a facemask with a clear plastic insert where her mouth was.

"Yes, Joshua Fletcher and Amy Brooks," Joshua confirmed.

"Please follow me."

Around the next corner, the woman opened a door. The first thing Amy saw was sunshine and a blue sky. As she walked through the door, she realized that they were outside now, leaving the sterile interior behind them. In the open space, she saw dozens of tiny houses. In between the cute, colorful cottages were walking paths, trees and bushes, and even a small creek winding its way through the grounds. The area reminded her of a resort in a foreign country. Not that she'd ever been to such a luxurious place, nor a foreign country.

"This way."

Amy turned to the woman who was directing them, and only realized now that she'd stopped walking. "What is this place?"

"It's a temporary housing center we built for the arrivals from 2025, for women like you."

Then she pointed to the path ahead of them, and Amy followed her, Joshua by her side. Along the path were fruit trees with signs inviting everybody to pick fruit for their consumption. She also saw smaller bushes with berries and the same inviting signs. At a tiny house that was labeled as *Pod 48*, they stopped. The woman opened the door and ushered them inside.

The moment Amy entered the pod, she felt a calmness come over her. This was more luxury than she'd ever expected. The large room was a living area with large floor-to-ceiling French doors leading to a small wooden terrace. The room was fully furnished and looked comfortable. To the left of the entrance was a small kitchenette.

"While you're in quarantine, your meals will be delivered to you three times daily. Just use your holocom to order what you want. Or you can use the built-in order screen on your TV."

Amy peered past a room divider. Behind it, she saw a king-sized bed and a door leading into an ensuite bathroom. This pod was larger than a regular hotel room. This was more like a suite in an expensive five-star hotel.

"You'll find clothing in various sizes in the bedroom closet, as well as all necessary toiletries. If you need anything else, just order it via Joshua's holocom or the TV set." She smiled. "The door to your pod will remain locked until your quarantine is over. Expect the results of your medical tests within the next twenty-four hours. If you haven't brought any infectious diseases with you, you will be free to roam around the grounds."

Then she turned directly to Amy. "Your orientation will begin the day after you're out of quarantine."

"Orientation? What do you mean?"

"You'll be introduced to life in 2085, so you can familiarize yourself with our technology, your rights as a global citizen, and be fitted with your own holocom. While you're going through the orientation and waiting for your holocom to be programmed, your Romeo may visit you at any time, day or night."

Panic rose inside her. "You mean, Joshua is leaving? And I'm staying here, alone?"

"During orientation, you'll be very busy. That's why we suggest that the Romeos leave to see their families, and make arrangements for your life together." She cast a look at Joshua. "If that's what you've both decided."

Joshua took her hand and squeezed it. "Don't worry, it'll be all right."

"Well," the woman said and headed to the door. "I'll leave you alone now. The results of your blood tests will be showing up on your TV screen as soon as they become available. If they're negative, the doors will unlock at the same time."

"And if not?"

"Then we'll bring you to a hospital to treat you. Don't worry, we'll take good care of you."

The woman left and closed the door behind her. A clicking sound echoed in the pod. The door to the outside world was locked.

Joshua saw the worry on Amy's face and couldn't really blame her. This was all new to her. Granted, he hadn't expected to be put in quarantine either, but he knew that this was done for everybody's health and safety and wasn't worried about it. He'd been aware that there would be routine medical tests upon their arrival, but not this, not a quarantine. To Amy, it might look like she was being imprisoned. It was his responsibility to calm her down and distract her so she wouldn't regret her decision of having traveled to his time.

"Baby," he said softly and pulled her into his arms. "Look at it this way: we're alone for the next twenty-four hours, and nobody will disturb us." He pressed a kiss to her forehead. "And we can order as much food and drink as we want." He winked. "No cooking involved."

She lifted her head. "I'm scared. In this time, I only know you. What if—"

He put a finger over her lips, guessing what she wanted to say. What if they didn't stay together, what if they weren't meant to be a couple? Then she would be all alone. "Everything will turn out all right. I promise you." He smiled at her. "Now, are you gonna kiss me, or have you decided to play hard to get?"

When her eyes lit up with joy, he knew he'd said the right thing. "Is that all you want? A kiss?"

He pulled her closer to him, and slid his hand to her backside to press her to his groin, where his cock was awakening. "I don't think a kiss is enough. I need a lot more than that."

"Tell me what you need," Amy teased, a coquettish glint in her green eyes.

Darn, she'd never looked more seductive. "I need to sink my cock into your hot pussy, because you make me so damn hard."

Amy slipped a hand between their bodies and laid it over his growing erection. "Yep. That's pretty hard."

He cocked an eyebrow. "Did you really have to check?"

"No, but why miss an opportunity to touch you?"

"You're taking the words right out of my mouth."

He lifted her into his arms and walked into the bedroom with her, while he took her lips and kissed her. Impatiently, he began to undress her, while Amy did the same to him. When they were both naked, Amy ripped her lips from his, breathing hard.

"Is it just me, or is it hot in here?"

"It is hot. It was April when we left 2025, it's July here. Besides, the planet is a few degrees warmer than what it was in your time. How about a shower?"

"Mmm. Together?"

"Absolutely."

He dragged her into the bathroom. He had to hand it to the Institute for Time Travel: they really knew how to make a newcomer feel welcome. The bathroom was downright luxurious, and the shower large enough for two people as if the institute expected the arriving lovebirds to use it together. But were he and Amy lovebirds?

Were they a couple? Would they last, or would the sexual fire that burned between them fizzle out quickly? He had to admit that sexually they fit perfectly. But would they fit as a couple? Would he be able to love her the way a man was supposed to love the woman who was willing to bear his children?

Maybe it was best to push these thoughts away for now and focus on what was immediately ahead of him: to make Amy feel good about her decision to come to the future with him. And that was something he knew he could accomplish, because he knew what she needed right now: to feel loved, even if he couldn't say the words. His actions would have to do.

He turned on the shower and set it to a cooler temperature, before he gave Amy a gentle shove. He followed her into the shower and pulled her into his arms, while the water rained down on them like the rain in a jungle.

He loved feeling her curves mold to his body, her chest rising and falling as she breathed, her hands caressing him, exploring him. Just like he explored her: first with gentle caresses, then with a more demanding touch.

Without a word, he turned her so she faced the shower wall. Amy laid her hands flat on it, while she took a step back so her ass was pointed in his direction.

"Is that how you want it?" she asked with a look over her shoulder.

"As if I could resist you." That was the truth. When it came to sex with Amy, he had no control, no power to deny her. "And just so you know: there are no condoms in 2085. This time, there won't be a barrier between us."

She gasped. "What if..."

"...if you get pregnant?" he finished her question for her. He slid one hand around her to touch her belly, and damn it, if he didn't feel a spark of excitement flare up inside him at the thought of his seed growing in Amy's body. Fuck! Why was he feeling like this? Could it be that maybe, just maybe, what he and Amy had was more than just sexual compatibility?

"Yes, what happens then?" she asked.

"I'll take care of you, no matter what." He grabbed her hips and adjusted his angle so his cock touched her pussy. "But right now, all I want you to think of is your pleasure. Just feel my cock and guide me to make you come. Can you do that?"

"Yes."

At her whispered word, Joshua thrust his erection deep into her. Her wet heat welcomed him, and her interior muscles imprisoned him. This felt even better than the times before, because this time the contact was skin on flesh.

"Fuck!"

He was glad that cool water ran down over their bodies, because his entire body stood in flames. No other woman had ever gotten him so hot. With every thrust into her delicious sheath, with every withdrawal, his tempo increased, and his breath quickened. Damn, if he wasn't careful, he'd come without warning. He tried to slow down, but he couldn't. All he could do was to make sure that Amy climaxed with him.

"Baby, tell me what you need," he begged.

"Touch me like you did sixty years ago."

That reply made him chuckle involuntarily, and gave him back a modicum of control.

"As you wish." He took one hand from her hip, and brought it to her pussy. He found her clitoris. Like he'd done the night before, he caressed her center of pleasure. Amy guided him with her hand on his, until he'd found the right rhythm and tempo.

"Oh, that's it, Joshua, oh, please..."

He concentrated on her movements until he felt her hold her breath, before a shudder went through her body. It reached his cock, and her interior muscles clamped around him. He let go of the last vestiges of his self-control and allowed his orgasm to wash over him. He felt his semen shoot into her, fill her and make his movements even smoother than before. He continued pumping into her, slower now, and gentler, while he continued to caress her clit.

"Joshua, but you've already—"

"Shh, baby, just let yourself go again. I love the way you squeeze me when you come."

His cock still semi-hard, he remained inside her while he rubbed his finger over her clit again and again until she orgasmed a second time.

Breathing hard, he leaned his head next to hers against the wall and allowed the water to cool his heated body.

"I think I might need a few minutes rest before we can repeat this," he murmured into her ear.

She chuckled in response. "Are you trying to prove something?"

He let out a breath. "Nope. I just can't get enough of this. You've turned me into a sex addict."

Though he was starting to think that sex wasn't the only thing he was becoming addicted to.

19
Heartbreak Hotel

Sunday, July 22, 2085

"Do you really have to leave?" Amy asked and looked at Joshua as he folded his jacket over his arm.

A half hour earlier, their test results had come back: they were both negative for infectious diseases. The door to their pod had unlocked.

He kissed her on the lips. "I have to go see my parents. But I'll be back soon. You'll be so busy with orientation that you'll barely notice that I'm gone."

"All right."

She watched Joshua leave the pod, and the door fell shut behind him. He was right, of course. She had to attend orientation. It was mid-morning, and Amy had already had breakfast with Joshua. The food was excellent here, healthy, and nutritious. When an employee had delivered their food the previous day as well as this morning, she'd been surprised at the quality and freshness of it. She'd never eaten that well in her life.

"Good morning, Amy."

At the sound of the voice, Amy spun around, but she was still alone in the pod.

"You're expected at the orientation in the outdoor meeting space A." She realized now that the voice was coming from a loudspeaker in the ceiling. "Please leave the pod and follow the signs to meeting space A."

A little apprehensive about having to face this new world on her own today, she left the pod and followed the signs posted along the footpath. Other women her age came out of their pods too and walked in the same direction. She didn't have to go far, until she reached an amphitheater, where many women had already taken a seat. At a small podium on the stage stood a woman. She wore a white lab coat. Behind her, a large movie screen showed a static image: *Welcome to 2085.*

Amy looked around and noticed that some of the girls had started chatting quietly. Amy took a seat on one of the benches, and watched as more and more girls filled the seats. A young woman sat down next to Amy and smiled at her.

"Hi, I'm Julie."

"I'm Amy."

"This is exciting, isn't it?" Julie asked, her face beaming.

"Yes," Amy admitted, though she didn't feel quite as carefree as Julie appeared to be.

"I can't wait for this orientation to be

over, so Carter and I can live together. He's picking me up the moment I've got my holocom."

Amy turned her face to the girl. She was beautiful, charming, and sweet. "Oh? I thought we had to stay here longer."

"I heard that's only the case if the guy who brought you here doesn't want to marry you. But Carter has already proposed." She smiled from one ear to the other. "He's gone to see his parents to get started on the wedding preparations. I can't wait."

Amy's heart pounded. She was happy for Julie, but also worried. Joshua hadn't once told her that he loved her or that he wanted them to be a couple. In fact, they'd both avoided the subject. Maybe it was just too early. After all, they hadn't spent six months with each other like the other couples had.

"I only met Joshua two weeks ago," Amy said. "We're still getting to know each other. I guess after six months together—"

"Oh," Julie said, "Carter and I have known each other for only a week, because something went wrong with his time jump, and he only arrived in my time a week before the outbreak of the virus. So we had to act quickly. But I guess, when you're right for each other, you don't need all that time."

Amy pasted a smile on her face. "Yeah, I suppose you're right." But did that mean that she and Joshua weren't right for each other? Did Joshua not have the same feelings for her as she had for him? Because even though she'd never told him that she loved him, she did.

She was glad to be interrupted by the person standing at the podium. "Welcome to 2085. I'm Eliza Dorchester, and I'm here to give you an overview of everything you need to know about your new lives."

Everybody fell silent.

"First and foremost, there's one very important thing you need to know. You have the same rights as every other citizen. You can choose your life partner freely. Nobody will force you to be with a man you don't love, even if that man saved you from dying in the 2025 pandemic by bringing you here. However, the same goes for the Romeo: he has no obligation to enter into a relationship with you or marry you."

Hushed murmurs travelled through the crowd. Amy's heart pounded out of control.

"And another important thing. I was young like you once, and I'm assuming that many of you have already had sex with your assigned Romeo. Should you find yourselves pregnant, but your Romeo isn't willing to commit to you, don't worry: we will take care of you. You will be able to raise your child without any financial worries. Healthcare is free in 2085, and we'll provide you with suitable accommodations. So, should you and your Romeo decide not to stay together, we'll help you with finding another partner, if you wish."

Amy let the words sink in as she thought back to the last twenty-four hours. She and Joshua had had unprotected sex more than just once. And she'd seen it as a sign that he wanted them to be a real couple. But what if that wasn't the case? Surely, he knew that the Institute for Time Travel would take care of her should she become pregnant. Was that why he'd told her not to worry?

Orientation day was interspersed with a break for lunch, where everybody assembled in a large tent where a delicious buffet was awaiting them. In the afternoon, more presentations by different people introduced the newcomers to the technology and customs of the 2080s. By late afternoon, Amy was exhausted from having to take in so much new information. She was glad when Mrs. Dorchester finally released them to return to their pods to rest before dinner.

Amy followed the footpath back to her pod. When she arrived there, a young woman her age stood waiting in front of it. She was the epitome of beauty: long blond hair, blue eyes, perfect skin, a stunning model-like body.

The woman looked her up and down, her gaze lingering on Amy's scarred face for longer than was polite. "Did you come to 2085 with Joshua?"

Amy nodded, curious. "Yes, I'm Amy." Was there something else on the agenda for today?

"Well," she said, smirking now. "I'm Kelly, and I'm Joshua's girlfriend. I just want to let you know not to expect him back."

Shock charged through Amy, and a gasp ripped from her lips. Joshua had a girlfriend while he'd slept with her? That couldn't be true. "But he—"

With an icy look, Kelly cut her off. "He only did his duty. I wasn't happy about him signing up for this program, but I forgave him. I suppose every man wants a last fling before he gets married." Then she pointed to Amy's scars. "And you didn't really think that a handsome man like Joshua could love a girl like you. Let me tell you something about Joshua: he likes to surround himself with pretty things. And you don't fit that category. He's out of your league. Maybe a guy who's desperate to have a family will take pity on you."

At the cruel words, tears welled up in Amy's eyes, but she pushed them down. She wouldn't give this heartless woman the satisfaction of seeing her cry. Still, the truth hurt. Joshua didn't want her. Despite everything that had happened between them, he'd only done his duty to his people. He'd brought her to the future with him. But he had no intention of spending this new future with her. She was on her own.

With her last ounce of control, she lifted her chin and looked straight into Kelly's cold eyes. "Don't worry. I only used him to make a better life for myself."

She turned away from Kelly and entered the pod, letting the door fall shut behind her. The tears started flowing the moment she was alone. She was in love with Joshua, but he was in love with somebody else.

20
Trouble in Paradise

Tuesday, July 24, 2085

Joshua hadn't seen or spoken to Amy since Sunday mid-morning when he'd left the Institute for Time Travel and returned to his parents' home. They'd been excited to have him home and were full of questions about his time in the past, and particularly about the woman he'd brought back. He'd told them about some of his experiences in 2025, but hadn't gone into detail about Amy, and hadn't mentioned her physical disfigurement. How could he answer their questions when he didn't know whether he had true feelings for her, or whether it was just sex that drew him to her? Just like it did now.

After nearly forty-eight hours without seeing her, without touching her, he felt like a drug addict on withdrawal. Fuck! He'd never felt like that when he hadn't seen Kelly in a few days. Was it because Amy was so much more generous, giving him free reign over her body when they made love? When he'd awoken with her in the pod on Sunday, he'd found Amy sucking his cock with such skill and abandon that he'd come so hard and so fast that he hadn't even been able to pull out of her mouth.

Just thinking of this now, made him yearn for Amy's touch. Damn it, he had to go and see her, even though he still had no answer to his ultimate question: could he fully commit to her and start a life with her, have a family with her? Maybe the answer to that question would reveal itself once they'd spent more time together, once they knew each other better.

He ordered a car to take him to the Institute for Time Travel. The gates of the institute were open now, which could only mean that quarantine had been lifted for all new arrivals. The women were allowed to receive visitors—not just their respective Romeos—and leave the compound if they wished to explore other parts of the city.

He took the footpath to Amy's pod and noticed that many young women were chatting with each other or walking hand in hand with young men, presumably the ones who had brought them to the future. There were signs posted for various events the women were requested to attend to learn more about the future. Other signs pointed to the communal dining tent. The entire place looked peaceful.

At the door to Amy's pod, Joshua took a deep breath. He opened the door quietly, because he wanted to surprise her. He found her standing in the living room, looking at the TV screen, which showed the agenda for the day. She wore shorts and a T-shirt.

"Amy," he murmured.

Amy spun around, and he was already opening his arms and walking toward her to embrace her, when she glared at him and took a step back.

"What are you doing here?"

The hostile tone in her voice made him stop in his approach. "What do you mean? I'm here because I missed you. I want to spend time with you."

She scoffed. "Right! What about your girlfriend? I suppose she doesn't have time today, or is she just not in the mood for sex? So you figured you could sneak in here for sex."

"What? I don't have a girlfriend."

"Stop lying to me, Joshua. She came to see me. Kelly—she told me you're getting married, and that I was just one last fling."

Fuck! He ran a hand through his hair,

trying to digest the news. "Kelly? She came here?" What the fuck! Why would Kelly claim that she was his girlfriend and they were getting married? She was engaged to Corbin Carmichael.

"It's not true, Amy. Kelly is my ex-girlfriend. And I have no idea why she would claim that we're getting married. She's engaged to somebody else."

He took a step toward her, but Amy lifted her hand to stop him. "Don't! Do you really think I'd let you touch me when you're just using me?" She shook her head. "How could I have been so stupid to think that you cared about me? It all makes sense now." She sniffled. "I met the other women from 2025. Their Romeos are committed to them. They are couples. But we're not! Because you only used me to do your duty, to bring me here. And I was so stupid to mistake sex for love."

"Please, Amy, I'm not with Kelly anymore. She lied. I don't know why. But I left her before I went back to 2025. We're not a couple anymore."

"Neither are you and I! Or can you tell me right here and right now that you want to spend your life with me? That you want to have a family with me?" Her voice broke. "That you love me?"

Joshua took a shaky inhale. Fuck! He couldn't lie to her. He wasn't ready to commit to her. But he didn't want her to think that he was just using her, because he wasn't.

"It's because of this, isn't it?" She turned her face so he had to look at the ugly scars.

He swallowed hard, not wanting to admit that her scars were still holding him back. "Please, Amy, give me some time."

"Just like I thought," she said, sounding resigned. "I'm not pretty enough for you. Go back to your girlfriend. She's forgiven you for cheating on her. And she's prettier than me. Then you don't have to worry about what people will say when they see you with me."

The words hit him in the gut. Amy had seen through him all along. She'd realized that her scars were still making him hesitate. But the thought of losing her suddenly frightened him. "Amy, you and I, we have something…"

There was a soft ping, then a voice came through the speakers. "Amy Brooks, please report to Laboratory H to be fitted with your holocom."

"It was only sex. Nothing more. Leave, Joshua. I don't want to see you anymore." She walked past him toward the door. "If you're still here when I'm back from my fitting, I'll have security remove you."

She left the pod. When the door fell shut behind her, Joshua stood there in the silence, his thoughts his only companion.

"We're not done, Amy," he murmured to himself. "Not by a long shot."

21
Blast from the Past

Getting the holocom fitted and going over the instructions of how to use it lasted about an hour. Amy was glad for the distraction. Looking into Joshua's eyes and seeing that he couldn't commit to her had hurt. And it would hurt for a long time. In a way, she blamed herself for falling for Joshua. When she thought back at every conversation they'd ever had, she could see clearly now that he'd never pretended that he loved her or that they would have a future together. She'd simply assumed it because physically, they'd been more than just compatible—they'd been perfect together.

But she couldn't just be a man's mistress, while he made a life with another woman, a much more beautiful one. Somehow, she had to survive this. Maybe one day, she would be ready to trust somebody else enough to allow herself to fall in love again. But right now, it was best to concentrate on her immediate future. One day at a time.

When she approached her pod, she noticed an old woman sitting on the bench outside. She was at least eighty years old, but looked healthy and strong in her loose-fitting navy pants and white blouse. She wore sunglasses, and her hair was almost white.

Amy walked toward the door to her pod, when the woman rose from the bench and addressed her.

"It's really you." She shook her head and smiled. "I've been waiting so long for this moment." She took off her sunglasses and slipped them into her pants pocket. "Amy..." Tears welled up in her eyes.

Amy stared at the woman. Her eyes reminded her of somebody. The voice had changed, but it was familiar too. Tears suddenly stung in her eyes, and she took a step closer. "Rosie?"

Rosie smiled and nodded, before she wrapped her arms around Amy and hugged her closely. "I've been waiting over sixty years for this moment."

"I can't believe you're here. How did you find me?"

Rosie released her from the embrace. "I have a friend at the Institute. He notified me when you arrived. You told me before you left to which year you'd be traveling with Joshua, so I made inquiries."

"Come, you have to tell me everything that happened after I left," Amy said. "Let's sit on the terrace."

When they sat down on the comfortable

outdoor two-seater-sofa on the small terrace of her pod, Rosie squeezed her hand. "I have to thank you for warning me about the pandemic. At first, I didn't want to believe you. But when the first people got sick in Los Angeles, just when and how you'd predicted, I knew what to do. I left L.A. My aunt had an old cabin in the San Bernardino mountains. I went there and stocked up on everything I would need for several months in isolation. It was hard to be alone for so long, but when I heard that everybody who worked at the Daily Grind got infected and several, including Mr. Mercola, died, I knew I'd made the right choice."

"Mr. Mercola died? I'm so sorry." Even though he hadn't been the best employer, she was sorry about his fate. "And your family? Your relatives?"

A sad smile traveled over Rosie's face. "Many died. I tried to warn them, told them to isolate, to avoid crowded places, to take precautions, but they didn't listen. Amy, if you hadn't warned me, I wouldn't have survived. I would have either been infected in the café or when visiting my family. And I would never have had this wonderful life."

"Tell me." Amy felt joy for her friend. "Did you get married?"

"Yes. And my husband is a wonderful man, still strong, still handsome. We have three children, and a dozen grandchildren. Even one great-grandchild already, and more on the way. They're all healthy, and because I never got infected with the 2025 virus, my offspring don't carry the mutated gene that makes women infertile."

"I'm so happy for you," Amy said, her voice breaking.

"I also understand now why you only told me about the pandemic and what year you were traveling to. Had you told me that the pandemic would create a gene mutation responsible for infertility, I would have been tempted to try and work on a cure decades before our scientists even discovered it. But then Joshua would have never traveled to 2025. And you wouldn't have met him. I would have destroyed your happiness."

Tears started running down her cheeks, and she couldn't hold back the sobs that ripped from her throat. There was no happiness, because Joshua didn't want her.

Rosie put her arm around Amy's shoulder and pulled her to her chest. "What's wrong, Amy? Don't cry. Everything turned out fine."

Amy lifted her head and looked at her friend. "Not for me. Joshua doesn't love me. He's going to marry Kelly, his girlfriend."

"That can't be," Rosie claimed. "They broke up before his trip to 2025, because Kelly accepted a marriage proposal from Corbin Carmichael. His family is very rich."

"How do you know about Kelly?"

"I might have kept an eye on Joshua ever since he was born." Mischief glinted in her eyes.

"You stalked him?"

"I don't think it's called stalking when it's done only to make sure nothing bad happens to him. I knew he had a girlfriend, but I also knew that Kelly was shopping for the richest husband. She has quite the reputation of being high-maintenance. I knew she would dump him for somebody richer so Joshua would be free to travel to 2025. I might even have manipulated the ride he ordered that evening when Kelly broke up with him, to make sure it took him to the Institute for Time Travel."

At Rosie's revelation, Amy had to shake her head. "How?"

"I have lots of friends and family. My son-in-law works for the company that provides the self-driving car service in Los Angeles."

"I can't believe you did all this. For me... Oh, Rosie..."

"I had to thank you somehow. Without you, I wouldn't be here today. I have a wonderful life, a loving family, a fulfilling job. All thanks to you."

"A job? You still work? I mean, you must be eighty-one by now."

"Eighty-two actually, but who's counting?" She smiled. "I'm a plastic surgeon. One of the best."

"I thought you were studying engineering back then."

"I was, but after the pandemic, after I realized that I would see you again in the future, I switched to medicine. I wanted to give back what you've given me." Rosie brushed her fingers over Amy's scarred face. "I developed a unique laser technique that can erase any and all scars. It's an outpatient procedure. It takes only a few hours, and the healing process is quick. In less than twenty-four hours I can make your face look flawless again."

Flawless? Amy let the words sink in. She could be beautiful again. No more disfiguring scars. Nobody would stare at her anymore. Joshua wouldn't reject her. She would be just as beautiful as Kelly. Would he choose her then? But if he did, would she ever really know if he truly loved her?

She knew the answer to it.

"If I do that, if I accept your offer, and Joshua comes back to me because of it, I could never be sure of his feelings for me. You understand that, don't you?"

Rosie nodded. "I understand."

"He has to love me with the scars, or not at all."

Rosie took her hands and squeezed them. "Then we have to find out why Kelly is suddenly back in the picture. You need to open Joshua's eyes so he can recognize that you're the right woman for him, not Kelly."

"How?"

Rosie winked and tapped on her holocom. "Let's see what Kelly's been up to since Joshua entered the time-travel program."

22
You're so Vain

Joshua rang the doorbell, and waited. But nobody was answering at the Shipley residence. He put his face to the glass door and shaded his eyes so he could see inside. Nobody appeared to be in the large living area, but he saw a movement beyond it, where the backyard and pool were located. He turned away from the entrance door and walked to the side gate that led onto the property. The gate wasn't locked, which wasn't unusual. Crime was extremely low in 2085, even in a large city like Los Angeles.

When he turned the corner of the house, he saw Kelly lounging near the pool. She was dressed in a bikini with a short sarong around her waist and hips. Her blond hair shimmered golden in the sun, and she looked just as beautiful as he remembered her.

He approached, and Kelly turned her head in his direction. Surprise flashed in her eyes, and a smile formed on her lips, as she stood up.

"Joshua," she murmured in that seductive tone she always employed when she wanted something.

"Kelly." He remained standing several feet away from her.

"You came." She took a few more steps toward him, her movements graceful and seductive. "I'm glad you're back." She put her hand on his chest and leaned in.

Joshua took her hand and pried it off him, before stepping back. "Don't."

Surprise flashed in her eyes once more, but this time it was laced with annoyance. "But I've forgiven you."

"Forgiven me?"

"Yes, for your little time-traveling fling. I'm not mad at you anymore."

Joshua narrowed his eyes. "You're not the one who has reason to be mad. I'm the one who's mad at you. What the fuck were you thinking harassing Amy and telling her lies about us?"

"Harassing? I wasn't harassing her. I was simply telling her the truth."

The anger inside him was close to boiling over. "And what truth is that?"

"That you're not going to marry her." She huffed. "I mean, why the hell would you marry somebody so ugly when you can have me?"

"You?" He shook his head. "May I remind you that you dumped me for Corbin Carmichael? Shouldn't you be planning your wedding, rather than feeding lies to my girlfriend?"

There, he'd said it. He'd called Amy his girlfriend, and it didn't feel like a lie. It felt right.

"But I'm free again, Joshua. I broke up with Corbin."

The news jolted him. Simultaneously, distrust rose in him. "Why?"

"Why do you think?" She approached him once more and now put both hands on his chest. "Because I realized that I didn't want Corbin. I love you."

When she leaned in for a kiss, he pushed her back. "You should have thought about that before you accepted his proposal. Did you know that I was gonna propose to you that night?"

"Oh, Joshua," she purred. "I'm so sorry. But now, I'm free again. I want you back."

He scoffed. "Yeah, well, *I'm* not free anymore."

Kelly's eyes widened. "You can't possibly want Amy. I mean, she looks grotesque!"

"I don't care what she looks like. She's a good person. A much better one than you. And we're good together. With her I can be myself. I don't have to play a role. And she cares about me."

Kelly huffed indignantly, her mouth turning into a thin line. "She doesn't care about you!" Her words were laced with poison. "You have no idea what she's really like. I didn't want to, but since you're too stubborn to see the truth, I'll have to do this." She tapped on her holocom. "This is what she said when I went to see her to find out if she had real feelings for you. I only wanted your best. I would have never tried to split you guys up, if I knew that she really cared about you. But she doesn't."

"Stop it, Kelly! You're just making things worse. I don't love you anymore."

"Listen, Joshua. Listen to this."

She tapped on the hologram hovering over her arm, and suddenly, he heard Amy's voice.

"Don't worry. I only used him to make a better life for myself."

It was Amy's voice. There was no doubt. But he knew she would have never said something like that. "How low are you prepared to go? This is a deep fake. Amy would never say something like that. She has a heart. She's a warm, loving woman. She's not like you."

Amy stepped out from behind the corner of the house where she'd heard the recording Kelly had played for Joshua.

"Yes, I said that," Amy said as she approached the two.

Both of them whirled toward her. Joshua stared at her in disbelief. There was hurt and disappointment in his eyes.

"I said it, because of the painful things that Kelly said to me. That you could never love anybody who looked like me. I was trying to protect myself. After all, you never told me that you loved me."

Joshua's gaze softened, and she knew he believed her. "Amy—"

"I was going to leave you be and accept that you don't want a life with me," she interrupted him, "but then a friend came to see me and told me what Kelly is really like."

"You bitch! Leave! Or I'm going to call the police," Kelly ordered.

But Amy shook her head. "No, I won't, not until I've said what I needed to say." She looked at Joshua again. "I couldn't have you run back to her for her to ruin your life. It doesn't matter if you're ever going to be with me, as long as you don't go back to her. She's no good for you. She's toxic. Ask her why she's not with Corbin Carmichael anymore and suddenly wants you back. Ask her."

Kelly's eyes widened, but she said nothing.

Joshua stared at her. "What happened with you and Corbin?"

Kelly didn't respond.

"Tell me, damn it!" When Kelly still didn't respond, Joshua turned back to Amy. "Amy?"

"Turns out that Corbin Carmichael figured out that Kelly was only using him too. She doesn't love him, nor you for that matter. Corbin ended the engagement and signed up for the time-travel program too. He's still in the past."

Kelly glared at her. "That's not true! I left him!"

Amy pointed at Kelly, then looked at Joshua. "Do you want somebody like her for a wife? Somebody who lies to you, and who'll trade you in for a richer guy first chance she gets?" She sighed. "That's all I wanted you to know."

She turned away.

"Amy," he called after her, but she didn't turn back.

She was following Rosie's advice. *Tell Joshua the truth about Kelly, and give him time to adjust. And if he really loves you, he'll come to you. Be patient.*

23
When a Man loves a Woman

Amy sat outside on the small terrace of Pod 48, and jumped up when she saw Joshua approach with a black woman and a white man, both in their fifties, following him. Her heart began to pound out of control. Had her action had the desired outcome?

Joshua stepped onto the terrace and stopped a few feet away from her.

"Amy," he murmured and ran his eyes over her, before gesturing to his companions. "I want to introduce my parents to you. Georgia and Marcus Fletcher."

Amy cast a hesitant look past him, a smile forming on her lips. There could only be one reason for him to bring his parents to meet her. Her pulse spiked.

"It's nice to meet you, Mr. and Mrs. Fletcher."

Joshua turned to his parents. "Mom, Dad, this is Amy. This is the girl I'm in love with." He looked back at her, meeting her eyes. "The girl I want to marry if she'll have me."

A gasp rolled over Amy's lips. Joshua wanted her. He wanted her, the ugly girl, when he could have taken Kelly back. It felt like she was in a dream. "Joshua..."

He reached for her hands and clasped them. "I would have never gone back to Kelly, even if you hadn't told me that she lied to me about Corbin." He reached up to her face and pulled a strand of hair away from the scarred side of her face, almost as if he wanted to emphasize that he truly saw her. "I'm sorry it took me so long to realize that I've been in love with you all along. I was a fool to focus on the outside, when I already knew who you really are on the inside."

Amy sniffled, unable to find the words. "Oh, Joshua..."

"Will you forgive me for being such a bone-headed idiot?"

She nodded. "Yes. Yes, of course." How could she not?

He grinned, then dropped onto one knee, while he pulled a small velvet box out of his pocket. Amy noticed his parents smile at the scene. At the same time, she saw several other people stop to watch them. Joshua didn't seem to mind. He glanced at them, and it looked as if he welcomed the witnesses. Her heart expanded.

"Amy, I love you with all my heart." He opened the velvet box and presented a ruby engagement ring to her. "Will you marry me?"

Amy pressed her hand to her mouth, still stunned. A sob escaped her lips, and with it her answer. "Yes! I love you, Joshua. I love you so much."

He slid the ring onto her finger, before he jumped up and pulled her into his arms. A moment later, his lips were on hers and he kissed her passionately. She heard dozens of people clapping. Joshua severed the kiss and looked at her. His chocolate brown eyes looked like molten lava.

"I love you, baby." Then he turned toward the crowd. "She said yes."

The people cheered, and his parents beamed with joy. She still couldn't believe what was happening. Joshua had really declared his love for her, and asked her to marry him. Not only that, he'd done it in public where everybody could witness whom he was choosing as his wife: not a beauty, but a girl with disfiguring scars. But right now, she didn't feel those scars, because the way Joshua looked at her made her feel beautiful and desired.

"Welcome to the family, Amy," Joshua's father said and opened his arms for a hug.

Joshua let go of her, and she accepted her future father-in-law's hug.

"Do I get to hug my future daughter too?" Joshua's mother asked with a smile.

She went from Joshua's father's arms to his mother's.

"Thank you," she said, her voice still choked up with tears of joy.

"We'd better get to planning the wedding," Joshua's mother announced. "When would you like to get married?"

"The sooner the better," Joshua said. He reached for her and pulled her back into his arms. "Right?"

"Yes."

"How about in three months?" Joshua's mother suggested.

"I was thinking more like in three days," Joshua said with a grin.

Amy stared at him in surprise. "So soon?"

"Yes. There's no reason to wait." He winked. "Besides, my mother is a whiz when it comes to organizing important events under deadline. Aren't you, Mom?"

His mother chuckled. "I do love a challenge. This Sunday it is."

Joshua noticed Amy's cheeks redden at all the attention their audience was paying them. His parents' warm smiles made his heart expand with joy. They accepted her, despite her disfigurement.

As the other people dispersed, Amy looked at her engagement ring. "It's so beautiful."

"It was my grandmother's," his mother said. "And it looks beautiful on you."

"I'll always treasure it, Mrs. Fletcher."

"Now, now, Mrs. Fletcher won't do at all. Call me Mom, or Georgia, whatever you prefer."

Amy appeared to hesitate for a moment, but Joshua nodded encouragingly.

"Thank you," she said, then added, "Mom." Tears suddenly ran down her cheeks, and Joshua hugged her to him.

"Then you'll have to call me Dad," his father insisted.

"Thank you, Dad," she said, her voice still laden with tears of joy.

His father put his arm around his wife's waist. "Honey, how about we give these two lovebirds a few hours alone? And then we'll go out for dinner together to celebrate?" He winked at Joshua.

"Excellent idea," his mother replied. "In the meantime, I'll put a few ideas for the wedding together." She smirked. "Any preferences for what you want your wedding to be like, Amy?"

Amy shook her head and looked up into his face. "It doesn't matter where it is or what it all looks like, as long as I'm with you, Joshua."

His parents laughed softly.

"You heard her, Mom," he said. "As long as it happens this weekend, I'm game for anything." He broke eye contact, and looked at his parents. "Thank you. We'll see you in a few hours?"

"You bet," his father replied, and they said their goodbyes.

When they were gone, he took Amy's hand. "How about you and I celebrate in private now?"

"I'd like that."

They entered through the sliding glass doors of the terrace and shut them. Joshua led her into the bedroom and pressed a button on the wall. As the blinds closed, he smirked. "For this part of our celebration, I don't want an audience."

"Neither do I." She put her arms around

him and pressed herself against him, her face only inches from his. "I love you, Joshua."

"I love you even more, Amy. I have the feeling we're going to be very happy together. And not just because sex with you is amazing."

She giggled.

"It's the truth," he whispered. "But there's so much more to you. With you I feel complete."

"Are you trying to make me cry again?" She sniffled.

"As long as they are tears of joy, I'll always welcome your tears." He pressed a soft kiss to her lips. "Now, how about you take off your clothes? I believe I haven't made love to you in over two days."

"Two very long days."

She reached for his T-shirt and pulled it over his head, before she opened the button of his pants. He stopped her from proceeding by snatching her tank top and pulling it over her head. Underneath it she wore no bra.

"Baby," he murmured, while he admired her naked breasts.

He touched them, taking both into his palms and kneading them. Amy moaned softly in response to his caresses. He felt her pull his zipper down and push his pants over his hips until they pooled around his feet. Before she could do the same with his boxer briefs, Joshua stopped her and freed her of her shorts and panties.

"Impatient much?" she asked with a smile.

"You would be too." He directed a pointed look at the outline of his erection as it stretched the fabric of his boxer briefs to capacity.

"I see. That definitely explains your impatience." She laid her palm over his hard-on and squeezed him through the fabric. The touch sent a spear of fire through his body.

Joshua gasped. "Damn it, careful with that, baby. Or it might go off too early."

But Amy didn't seem to be deterred by his warning and instead, hooked her thumbs underneath the fabric and stripped him. He helped and stepped out of his shoes so he could free himself fully of his clothes.

Naked, he pulled her into his arms, her body molding to his. He loved the way she felt, the skin-on-skin contact, the intimacy of their embrace. And the knowledge that she was his to love and to cherish.

Joshua captured her lips and explored her. He lifted her off her feet and carried her to the bed, where he lowered them down on the sheets without severing the kiss or the embrace.

Amy spread her legs without his urging, and he slid into the space she'd made for him, his cock already poised at her pussy.

He ripped his lips from hers. "Fuck, I promised myself to go slower this time."

"Slow is overrated." She put both hands

on his ass, and drew him to her, his cock parting her nether lips.

"You have a way of talking me into it that's hard to resist."

"Then don't resist."

Joshua didn't wait for her last word to roll over her lips and thrust into her to the hilt. She gasped. He loved how tight she was, how she fit around him. Simply perfect.

Joshua began to move, and she moved with him, joining his rhythm. They moved in sync their bodies merging. They were connected, not just by his cock inside her pussy, but by the love that lived in their hearts, a love that would grow even stronger with the years.

Everything felt more real now. Their lovemaking was more intense, almost raw and untamed, without barrier, without holding back. He was finally ready to give everything of himself to this woman, because the woman in his arms gave him everything in return: her heart, her body, and her soul.

When Amy's breathing became more ragged, he knew they were both close, and he increased the tempo of his thrusts.

"Yes, Joshua, yes..."

He shifted his angle just slightly, so that with every thrust, he brushed over her clit. Amy's interior muscles suddenly spasmed around him as she climaxed. She squeezed his cock like a tight glove, and he came without warning. He felt his semen shoot through his cock and fill her, and the thought that they could create a new life at any time made his heart leap with excitement.

"You little minx," he murmured, as he stopped moving and remained braced on his elbows and knees. "One of these days, I'll teach you how enjoyable it is to go slowly."

Amy grinned mischievously. "It was pretty enjoyable already."

"Are you making fun of me?"

"I wouldn't dare." But a giggle escaped her lips.

"I guess I'm gonna have to silence you."

Before she had a chance to respond, he kissed her. He loved that she seemed more confident now, and he knew that he would do everything in his power so she would never doubt his love for her, never feel as if she wasn't worthy. Because she was precious.

24
Beauty and the Beast

Sunday, July 28, 2085

Joshua stood at the head of a small platform that had been erected at the Culver City beach not far from his parents' house. He was dressed in white linen pants and a Hawaiian shirt, both of which he'd found in a second-hand store, rather than the dark suit customary for a wedding. Amy had wanted something simple, something that reminded her of the time she was from, and he was more than happy to comply.

On the planks that were made to look

like wood, stood two dozen chairs decorated with seasonal flowers and pink bows. His parents sat in the front row, beaming proudly. His cousins, aunts and uncles had also come, as well as his closest friends from college.

He looked toward the tent that had been erected just beyond the beach, knowing that Amy would eventually emerge from there. He hadn't seen her since Friday morning, when he'd left the temporary housing complex of the Institute for Time Travel. She'd told him that there were so many things she had to do before the wedding that it was best if she spent the last two nights as a single woman on her own. He hadn't really understood why, but he'd given into her wishes, knowing that soon they would be spending every night together in the house that his parents were giving them as a wedding present.

His father had offered to walk Amy down the aisle, but she had declined saying that she had somebody who would do that. Even though Joshua had been curious who she was talking about, she'd only said that it was a surprise.

At a movement at the tent, Joshua focused his eyes. Amy emerged in a long, white wedding dress with a wide skirt and an embroidered tight shoulder-free bustier. A grey-haired woman in her seventies or eighties walked next to her. She was dressed in a blue-green-pastel-colored dress. Joshua had never seen the woman. When the two reached the path that led from the grassy area around the tent to the small platform that had been erected over the sand, Joshua could finally see Amy's face. His heart stopped.

"Amy?" he murmured to himself and made an involuntary step toward her.

Amy simply smiled at him and continued walking toward him. With every step she took he got a clearer look at her. She was beautiful. It wasn't just the dress and the way her hair was braided with tiny flowers that made her look like she was stepping out of a fairytale, no, it was more: her face was flawless. Where just a few days ago, ugly scars had marred her face, he saw only beautiful, perfect skin.

Amy stopped near the front row where his parents were sitting, and the older woman who'd walked with her sat down next to his mother. Amy continued walking and stopped right in front of him, beaming.

He lifted his hand to verify that he wasn't hallucinating. "Your scars, they're gone." Her skin felt as smooth as a baby's.

Amy cast a glance back to where the older woman was sitting, then looked back at him. "My friend Rosie did this for us. She's a plastic surgeon."

"How? I don't understand. How did you know about her?"

"Don't be mad at me, but I knew Rosie from the café. I warned her about the pandemic before we left, and she survived because of it. And I told her that you were taking me to the year 2085, but I didn't tell her about the infertility gene, because I knew if I did, it would have changed the future, and you might have never traveled back to find me." She cast a quick glance at Rosie, then looked back at him. "Rosie became a plastic surgeon because she wanted to thank me. She waited all these years for me to arrive in the future."

"Oh Amy! Of course, I'm not mad." He pulled her to him. "But you know that you didn't have to do this for me. I love you no matter what."

She smiled. "I know. But I couldn't turn down a wedding present from Rosie, could I?"

"No, that would be impolite." He couldn't help himself and caressed her face before kissing her deeply. "Now you're as beautiful on the outside as you are on the inside." He turned his head toward Rosie and locked eyes with her. "Thank you, Rosie, thank you for this gift."

Rosie smiled and nodded. Then she made a motion toward the officiant who waited to perform the ceremony. "I was promised to witness a wedding."

His parents laughed with tears in their eyes.

"Yes," Joshua said and turned to Amy. "Let's get married, baby. I love you."

"I love you, Joshua, forever and always" Amy replied, her green eyes shining back at him with love and adoration.

He couldn't imagine a better future than the one he was starting now, with Amy by his side, a future filled with joy and laughter, with love and affection, a future they would have never had if he hadn't traveled back in time to find her.

About the Author

Tina Folsom was born in Germany and has been living in English speaking countries since 1991. Tina has always been a bit of a globe trotter. She lived in Munich, Lausanne, London, New York City, Los Angeles, San Francisco, and Sacramento. She has now made a beach town in Southern California her permanent home with her American husband and her dog.

She's written over 50 romance novels in English most of which are translated into German, French, Italian, and Spanish.

https://tinawritesromance.com
tina@tinawritesromance.com

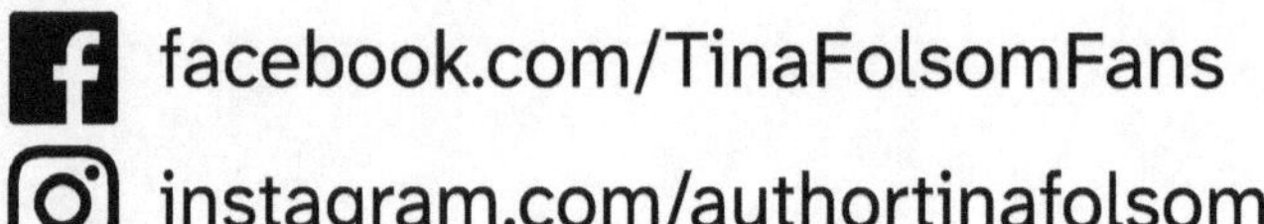
facebook.com/TinaFolsomFans

instagram.com/authortinafolsom